Marina Oliver has published almost fifty novels under various pseudonyms, plus half a dozen non-fiction books. She has written historical novels as well as twentieth century sagas, contemporary romances and crime.

Marina was the Chairman of the Romantic Novelists' Association and also lectured in America and on Cunard cruise ships. She has edited magazines and novels and runs many writing courses and workshops.

Marina now splits her time between rural Shropshire and Madeira and is married with four children and several grandchildren.

For more details on the author visit Marina's website: www.marina-oliver.net

SUPERVISING SALLY

Phoebe is delighted to go to Brussels as companion to Sally, rather than be an unpaid governess to her sister Jane's children. Her hopes are dashed when Zachary, Earl of Wrekin, claims Phoebe is too young for the task, and refuses to escort her. She finds herself unable to control the rebellious Sally, who gets into many scrapes even before they leave London. However, when Phoebe rescues Sally from a calamitous action, Zachary relents. But Jane's husband and his unpleasant sisters cause irritation on the journey. Then Napoleon escapes from Elba and everything is in turmoil for Phoebe.

Books by Marina Oliver
Published by The House of Ulverscroft:

HIGHLAND DESTINY
CAVALIER COURTSHIP
LORD HUGO'S BRIDE
THE BARON'S BRIDE
RUNAWAY HILL
MASQUERADE FOR THE KING
LORD HUGO'S WEDDING
CAMPAIGN FOR A BRIDE
RESTORATION AFFAIR
COURTESAN OF THE SAINTS
THE ACCIDENTAL MARRIAGE
A DISGRACEFUL AFFAIR

MARINA OLIVER

SUPERVISING
SALLY

Complete and Unabridged

ULVERSCROFT
Leicester

First published in Great Britain in 2009 by
Robert Hale Limited
London

First Large Print Edition
published 2010
by arrangement with
Robert Hale Limited
London

The moral right of the author has been asserted

British Library CIP Data

Oliver, Marina, *1934 –*
    Supervising Sally.
    1. Europe- -History- -*1789 – 1815*- -Fiction.
    2. Voyages and travels- -Fiction. 3. Historical fiction.
    4. Large type books.
    I. Title
    823.9′14–dc22

    ISBN 978–1–44480–177–4

Published by
F. A. Thorpe (Publishing)
Anstey, Leicestershire

Set by Words & Graphics Ltd.
Anstey, Leicestershire
Printed and bound in Great Britain by
T. J. International Ltd., Padstow, Cornwall

This book is printed on acid-free paper

1

Phoebe Kingston looked across the bed at her sister with a mixture of amusement and irritation. It was just like Jane to arrive and start issuing orders. She had always been like that, but since her marriage had become even more autocratic.

Jane Bradshaw was tall and had been stately as a girl. Now, approaching her thirty-fourth birthday, she had grown stout and regal. She favoured highly embellished gowns in dark colours, puce, pewter and chocolate being her favourites. The stoutness could be ascribed to her presenting her husband with six pledges of her affection within little more than twelve years, but Phoebe thought it might also have something to do with the large meals her husband Reginald, a Yorkshire mill owner, demanded.

Phoebe herself was tall, but slender. The sisters both had dark hair which refused to curl. How their fair-haired, diminutive, delicate mother and red-haired father had produced two such tall dark daughters was a mystery. Both, they were told, took after Dr Kingston's father.

Mrs Kingston, lying in the bed, was so tiny she barely raised the blankets. She spoke now, in a hoarse whisper. 'I knew you would help us, Jane.'

'Well, of course. Reginald and I always meant to help you after Papa died, but you wanted to be independent. I would have come earlier but for my lying-in. I came as soon as I could safely leave little Hubert with his wet-nurse. Reginald's sisters are quite capable of dealing with the servants, though they are not as strict as I am. However, as soon as you are well enough for the journey, I will take you to Yorkshire. We have an excellent doctor and I will hire a competent nurse.'

Phoebe pressed her lips together tightly. She would not rise to Jane's provocation. Did she think they had no good doctors here in Buxton? And as for a nurse, none could have cared for her mother with the same devotion she had used during the past two months.

Mrs Kingston had contracted a chill in September, which had turned to an inflammation of the lungs, and was only just recovering. Dr Watkins had praised Phoebe for her dedication, and said that without her Mrs Kingston would not be alive today. The medicines she had needed, and the invalid food, had eaten into their tiny income, however, and it had been to save her mother fretting about how they would manage that Phoebe had written to Jane to ask if she would invite Mrs Kingston to stay with her for a few months.

She had not, however, anticipated Jane's response that they must both come and make their home with the Bradshaws.

'You are living here in two rooms, since you had to give up Papa's house. How can you entertain your friends properly in such inferior lodgings? And look at your clothes — they are not at all fashionable.'

Since Jane's clothes were anything but fashionable, according to what Phoebe had seen in even last year's copies of *La Belle Assemblée*, given them by a friend, she ignored this slur. Jane automatically disapproved of everything Phoebe did, ignoring their straitened circumstances.

'All our friends are here in Buxton,' she protested. 'We could never entertain them at your home. The rooms may be small, but we are content.'

'You will soon make new acquaintances. We have a wide circle amongst the Yorkshire gentry and mill owners, and we entertain regularly, for Reginald's commercial interests, you know. As for being content, how can you be without some of the refinements of life?

You cannot even afford to pay for the subscription library, or attend the theatre or concerts.'

'We could before Mama was ill and needed so many medicines.'

Jane snorted. There really was no other word to describe it, Phoebe thought, suppressing her sudden desire to laugh. Jane was eleven years older and had dominated the nursery and schoolroom. When she married, ten-year-old Phoebe had celebrated by making a bonfire of every possession Jane had left behind her. Clothes, books, sketch books and painting materials had all been heaped on the smouldering embers of the gardener's bonfire, and it had been stirred to glorious life. Phoebe had been discovered capering round it, chanting what she fondly imagined were magic incantations against Jane's ever returning, and tossing the leaves of Jane's diaries on to the flames.

Her punishment had been severe. Papa had never previously thrashed her, and the longest she had ever been confined to her room on bread and water had been a day. The week of solitary confinement during which she had nursed her bruises had, she defiantly maintained, been worth every minute.

Jane, when told of the wickedness, had claimed to forgive her, but in the thirteen

4

years since had rarely let any meeting pass without some reference to it. If she had not teasingly thanked Phoebe for destroying her diary's youthful indiscretions, it had been a laughing reminder that Reginald had been forced to buy new clothes for her on their return from their wedding journey.

'When will Mama be fit to travel?' Jane now asked Phoebe, when they left their mother to sleep and had retreated to the drawing-room. 'I do not wish to leave Reginald and the children for long. And it would be better if you could be settled before the Christmas festivities.'

'Dr Watkins says she must not travel for at least another two weeks.'

'I cannot remain here for so long a time. If the weather is clement I will send the carriage for you in two weeks, with a maid I can trust to help you if I have not by then hired a nurse. Fortunately it is only forty or so miles, and if you start early you can do it in a day, while taking it easy for Mama's sake. But my coachman can be trusted to take good care of you.'

'Thank you, we are grateful,' Phoebe said. She had to be. There was no alternative, and if her mother wished to remain in Yorkshire it would certainly ease their dire financial situation. Until her illness they had, with care, managed on the tiny income her father had left them. Perhaps her mother would not find it as irksome as she would to be forever grateful to Jane and Reginald, and expressing this gratitude in suitable terms every day.

'It is my duty,' Jane said. 'As for you, Phoebe, you can help me by teaching the children. Their governess has given notice, the ungrateful wretch. Just because I asked her to teach Mary, when she said she had only been hired to teach Reggie and Anne. As though a three-year-old made any difference! And the older boys are at school during term time, but she objects to looking after them during the holidays.'

Phoebe gulped. She had always hated the idea of being a governess, but to be such to Jane's children, spoilt brats as they were, would be intolerable. 'What salary are you offering?' she asked.

'Salary? Don't be ridiculous. How can I pay a salary to my own sister? When I offer you and Mama a home the least you can do to repay me is help with the children.'

★ ★ ★

Relishing her Lady Bountiful role, Jane sent Phoebe shopping the following day, instructing her to purchase the items on the list she had written, and nothing else.

'The money should be sufficient, if you are careful not to be cheated. Keep a record of what you spend on each item.'

Phoebe seethed with annoyance. As if she had not been doing the marketing for the past four years, since her father had died so unexpectedly after a fall from a horse. If anyone knew how to stretch the pennies she did. Donning her old pelisse, which Jane had sneered at, and her much-darned gloves, she managed to leave the house without replying. An argument would upset her mother, who had been allowed to get up and sit beside the fire in the drawing-room.

Could she endure to live with Jane? After only one day she was feeling hurt, angry and resentful of her sister. She had no desire to teach young children, and from what she knew of Jane's brood, they were sly, whining creatures. She was not surprised their governess had left.

What alternative did she have? Becoming a governess in some other household would be preferable, and at least she would be paid for her efforts. Or she might become a companion to an elderly lady. There were plenty of these living in Buxton, or who visited to drink the waters. Perhaps she should visit one of the registries and enquire

7

about openings. She knew she was temperamentally unfit for either position, but she could, she decided rather bleakly, curb her natural high spirits and behave with decorum. That was something she could not do in Jane's household. Her sister managed to annoy her with almost every word.

Mama would be hurt, and would not understand. Since Papa's death she had clung to Phoebe, and become withdrawn. She still met her oldest friends occasionally, but she was no longer lively, keenly appreciating the ridiculous, laughing with Phoebe at the exaggerated dress some of the dandies wore.

Phoebe sighed. Would it be better to find herself a position now, rather than come to blows with Jane, something she knew would be inevitable if they lived together, and leave then? At least if she left now, they could remain on good terms, she hoped. Jane would be offended initially that Phoebe had rejected her children, but that would soon pass.

She was deep in these thoughts when a lady passing by touched her arm. She was in her thirties, a small, slightly plump woman with short, curly brown hair and sparkling hazel eyes. Elegantly dressed in a dark-blue fur-trimmed pelisse, close-fitting dark-blue hat, and carrying a sable muff, she looked warm and comfortable, unaffected by the sharp wind which was blowing Phoebe's thin pelisse around.

'Phoebe, my dear.'

'Lady Drayton! I didn't know you were back in Buxton.'

Beatrice, Lady Drayton was an old friend of her mother's who lived near Jane in Yorkshire. Her husband was elderly and had rarely left his home in the past few years.

'We arrived at our town house two days ago. Lord Drayton needs to consult Dr Watkins, and I need some new gowns, since we are having a large house party for Christmas, and my wardrobe is sadly out of date. I intended to call on your mother, but I heard she was ill. Not serious, I trust?'

'She is recovering. She was very ill for some weeks, but Dr Watkins has been very good.'

Lady Drayton nodded. 'He is one of the best doctors here, but nothing like your dear father. He was the only one who could cure Lord Drayton when he had that persistent ulcer. Is your mother well enough to receive visitors?'

'I'm sure she would love to see you, Lady Drayton. You were such a good friend when Papa died, helping us to find accommodation. But we will be going to Yorkshire in two weeks, if Mama is well enough to travel.'

'Yorkshire?' Lady Drayton looked concerned. 'It's not a good time of year to travel over the Peak if your mother is at all frail.'

'I know, but Mama wants to go, and Jane will send her carriage. We will be quite comfortable.'

'So you are going to stay with Jane for a while. I heard she had another son. This is the fourth, is it not?'

'It is. Reginald will have plenty of heirs for his mills. But we are going to live with them.'

Lady Drayton raised her carefully plucked eyebrows. 'Live with Jane and her family? Forgive me, child, but will you enjoy that?'

Phoebe laughed ruefully. 'No, I will not, especially as she intends me to take the place of her children's governess, who has just given notice.'

'I cannot see you as a governess, my dear,' Lady Drayton said, and Phoebe's determination to avoid such a fate strengthened.

'Well, I have to become that, or a companion. I would rather work for someone who will pay me, however.'

'You mean Jane will not give you a salary?'

'She believes giving us a home is sufficiently generous.'

Phoebe paused. Here was an opportunity that might not come again. Lady Drayton knew lots of people, was well connected, part of a large family. She might be able to help.

'Lady Drayton, do you know of anyone who needs a companion? I think I would prefer that to teaching children.'

'I will think about it. I will come and see your mother in a few days. Do give her my best wishes for a full recovery.'

★ ★ ★

Zachary Walton, Earl of Wrekin, handed his hat and riding gloves to her ladyship's maid when she opened the door of their suite at the Old Hall.

'Thank you, Turner. Is my sister in?'

'Yes, my lord. I will bring some Madeira.'

He nodded, and knocked lightly on the parlour door, before walking in. Beatrice rose from her escritoire, where she had been writing letters, smiled at him, and came across the room to reach up and kiss him on the cheek.

'Zachary, you made good time. It's good to see you after so long. You look well. Can you stay?'

'A night only, I'm afraid, then I have to go to London. I expect to be sent to Brussels soon after Christmas, and there are many things to arrange first. But I will make sure I come to Ridgeway Park for your party.'

'Brussels?' Beatrice looked thoughtful as she sat down again, and Zachary grinned at her. What was she plotting now? Beatrice was five years older than he, but they had always been good friends, except when she tried to force him to do things he objected to, like make offers to her young acquaintances. When he finally married, and he knew that one day he must, he intended to choose his own bride, not have one foisted on him by his sister, however fond of her he was.

'Not everyone is in Vienna at the Congress,' he said, and she laughed. 'There is some diplomatic activity going on elsewhere too, and perhaps more successfully than with those laggards in Vienna.'

'I do know. My sister-in-law's husband is there.'

'Sir William Benton? I heard he had some new diplomatic duties. Do you wish me to take him your good wishes?'

'Not precisely. I wish you to take him his daughter.'

'I beg your pardon?' What was Beatrice up to now? 'Is she another of the damsels you keep thrusting under my nose?'

'Oh, by no means! Sally Benton is too young for you. She's only seventeen, and a handful. That's why her mother wants to be rid of her.'

He clasped his brow theatrically and staggered to collapse onto a chair by the window. 'I think you'd better explain.'

Beatrice laughed. 'Sally's mother, Clara, is busy remodelling Benton Manor. You know she inherited a fortune from her godfather?'

'Yes, but William is rich enough to do up his own house if he wants to, without that.'

'Clara and William do not, I'm afraid, have a great deal in common. They have lived separate lives for the past ten years, since she produced her son. He is happy for her to entertain herself with architectural improvements while he moves in diplomatic circles.'

'Hasn't he recently returned from Brazil?'

'Yes, and he is now in Brussels.'

'But why must Sally go there?'

'Her governess has retired, and Sally is a handful.'

'I do recall some outrageous pranks when she was younger, and visiting you and Gregory.'

'Clara is unwilling to leave her architects and present Sally this coming Season, and she told me she felt it was time William took a hand in rearing her. With him fixed in Brussels, and as most of the polite world seem to have transferred themselves there, or to Vienna, it provided her with an ideal opportunity.'

Zachary frowned. 'You almost make me feel sorry for Sally. Does her father want her?'

'I'm sure he doesn't, her presence will severely cramp his style. He has a reputation with the ladies, you know.'

'Yes, I do,' Zachary replied, recalling some of the more deplorable stories circulating in the clubs. 'Can't he refuse to have her?'

'Clara has threatened to prevent young Frederick from visiting his father during his summer holidays if he refuses to have Sally.'

'William sounds like a puny sort of fellow if he puts up with that.'

'He is the sort of man who prefers a peaceful life without domestic strife.'

'Then he should never have married Clara! It sounds as though Sally takes after her mother.'

'He did marry her, and has to live with it.'

'If you say so. But what is this about my escorting Sally to Brussels? It's impossible! Think of the scandal of the two of us travelling together.'

'But you would not be alone with her. I can provide Sally with a companion she will like, and she will have her maid. You will have your valet. You will be quite a large party.'

He shook his head. He should have known Beatrice better. 'You have it all planned, I see, and it's pointless my arguing. Very well, I'll bear lead Sally to Brussels, but I will have no more to do with her once I have handed her over to her father. Was that what you wanted me to say?'

'Dear Zachary, I knew I could depend on you.'

★　★　★

Mrs Kingston held out her hand and smiled. She was a small woman, still pretty, but ill health had faded her looks. Her gown was an old favourite, the skirt wider than fashionable, but it was neat, and she had a warm if old Paisley shawl about her shoulders.

'Do forgive me for not rising, Lady Drayton.'

'Of course you must not. I know you have been very ill, and I came to see how you were.'

'Much better, thank you. That dreadful cold and cough have gone, thank goodness, but I still feel dreadfully weak from being confined to bed for so long, unable to take my usual walks.'

'Phoebe tells me you are going to live with Jane in Yorkshire. Your friends in Buxton will miss you.'

Phoebe thought she saw a shadow cross her mother's face. 'I'll miss them too, but it seems best for everyone if I accept Jane's kind invitation and go to live with her and her family. The past few weeks have been difficult for Phoebe with so much extra to do, looking after me.'

'Mama, you know I haven't minded.'

'You've been very good to me.'

Beatrice smiled at her. 'Well, at least we can see you often there. Ridgeway Park is only ten miles away from Bradshaw Towers, and maybe you could spend some time with us. I rarely go away now, with Lord Drayton preferring to remain at home most of the time. It does not seem fair to leave him for more than a few days.'

'We'd be very grateful. You have always been good to us.'

'I will be going away for a few weeks in the New Year, though. I've come with an ulterior motive this time, I have to confess. Lord Drayton's niece, Sally Benton, is to go to visit her father in Brussels for a few months. I am hoping you will permit Phoebe to accompany her as a companion.'

Phoebe gasped. She had made enquiries at the Buxton Registries, but they had not been optimistic about her chances of obtaining employment. She looked too young, they said. One lady had sniffed and said she was too pretty; employers would be afraid young and impressionable male relatives would be too taken with her. She was resigned to going to Yorkshire in a few days' time, and pessimistic about her chances of finding a suitable position from there. This would be a reprieve.

'To Brussels? So far away?' Mrs Kingston said, her voice doubtful. 'But is it safe?'

'It's been safe for six months, since that monster abdicated. You need not worry about Phoebe. She would be well taken care of. Sally will have a maid to accompany her, an older woman who has known her all her life. My brother will be in charge of the party, but first, I was intending to take both girls to London immediately after Christmas to buy clothes. Sally will have nothing suitable, as she has lived all her life in the country. And I will buy whatever Phoebe needs. We intend to pay her a good salary, too.'

The amount she mentioned made Phoebe gasp again. It was far more than they had told her to expect at the registries.

'Phoebe can escort you to Yorkshire, spend Christmas with you, and I will send a carriage for her so that we can travel to London together and pick up Sally on the way. Her home is in Oxfordshire. Well, Phoebe, will you oblige me by helping me with my niece?'

17

* ★ ★ ★

There were very few people in London, Zachary discovered, when he dined at his club on the evening he reached town. Most had retreated to their country estates for Christmas or were guests at houses of friends. Only those whose business kept them in London, or who detested the country, remained. One of the latter was Hester, Lady Mickleton. He had found a scented note from her when he arrived at his rooms, and spent the dinner hour wondering whether to accept the invitation enclosed. If he did, she might take it as encouragement, and he did not wish to permit their dalliance to develop into an affair.

Lady Mickleton had, he was well aware, had several lovers previously. She was a petite blonde, twenty-eight years old but with the aid of cosmetics pretending to be eighteen. Married to a man more than twice her age, she had produced the required heir within a year of her marriage, but the boy was kept in seclusion in their Northumberland castle, where Sir George also spent much of his time.

Zachary had enjoyed their light-hearted flirtation, but two considerations gave him pause before he allowed it to progress. He suspected Hester could become an intense and demanding mistress, and he had great admiration for Sir George, who had been a most successful soldier before being badly wounded at Vimeiro. He did not want to deceive an honourable man. If Sir George had himself taken mistresses, the situation would be different, but Zachary had never heard a word about any infidelities.

In the end, knowing there would be several other people at the card party, he decided to go. He would be able to judge whether Hester was becoming impatient, and if so, he would distance himself from her. It would be a pity, but he would not lack female companionship. There were always bored wives and widows willing to flirt with personable men.

Lady Mickleton lived in Mount Street, and he was soon being admitted to the drawing-room, where he found a dozen or so people chatting. Lady Mickleton came forward to greet him, clasping his hands in hers, and enveloping him in a cloud of eau de nil.

'You naughty man! You left town without telling me you were going to be away! I've been pining for you. But now you are back, for a long time, I hope.'

'I'm afraid not. I'm promised to my sister in Yorkshire for Christmas,' he said, smiling down at her, then disengaged his hands and turned away to greet the other guests.

They were soon occupied at the card tables, but when there was a break for supper, Lady Mickleton came and sat beside Zachary.

'I'm going home for Christmas too,' she said. 'It's so long since I've seen little George, and I really must keep an eye on his new tutor. Sir George doesn't know how to tell whether he is doing his job adequately. Perhaps you could escort me as far as Ridgeway Park? And I haven't seen dear Beatrice for years. I detest travelling alone, innkeepers are never as helpful as when there is a man to take charge.'

Zachary heard warning bells. 'I'm sorry, Hester, but I won't be able to leave until a few days before Christmas, and when I do I will have to travel faster than you would like. It would not allow you enough time to reach home before Christmas.'

She pouted. 'Oh, I understand. You don't want my company. But you'll be back in London in January, as I will. I know I won't be able to endure Northumberland for more than a week or two. I'll see you then.'

He was about to tell her he was soon to go to Brussels, but bit back the words. Better to let her discover it for herself, after he had gone. The hint should be enough to warn her of his waning interest.

★ ★ ★

With London and Brussels to look forward to, Phoebe contrived to keep her temper during the time she spent with the Bradshaws. Jane's disapproval of the plan washed over her, and when Reginald Bradshaw remonstrated with her, telling her she was an ungrateful and undutiful daughter for deserting her mother, she simply smiled at him and assured him that she knew her mother would be perfectly content living with him and Jane.

'And your delightful children,' she added, just as the two eldest boys, home from school for the holidays, waving wooden swords and shrieking warlike chants, rushed into the drawing-room and began chasing each other round the furniture.

Why, she wondered, when Jane was so determined to order everyone else's life, did she not do more to control her children? At least Lady Drayton's offer had released her from the dreaded prospect of trying to teach them.

Bradshaw Towers was a grim, grey house on the edge of the moors. Built of dark-grey stone, it was square, three storeys high, with what Phoebe thought were silly, useless little turrets stuck on at each corner, giving the house its pretentious name. They were about the size of a closet, and as far as she knew had never been used for any purpose. The house was furnished lavishly but with little taste. If something gleamed with polish, was new and expensive, or was embellished with gold or silver, it had Reginald's approval. Little had changed since Phoebe's last visit after her father had died. That had been in winter too. The moorland scenery had, she was forced to admit, a certain bleak grandeur, but she would not like to live there all the time. When they had been invited to visit soon after Jane's marriage, Phoebe had escaped as often as she could, walking on the moors. In summer it had been better, she thought, but not a great deal.

One day she had explored southwards, climbing a long ridge a few hundred yards from the house, and looked down in astonishment at a long, winding valley. There was a huddle of huge buildings following the course of the river, and belching out smoke, and surrounding them a maze of narrow streets spreading up the sides of the valley, lined with terrace upon terrace of tiny houses.

'The mills all belong to Reginald,' Jane had explained when she asked about it. 'I never go there. It's dirty and unpleasant. Reginald's father built this house behind the ridge so that he would not have to see it, or hear, or smell it.'

'The people who work in the mills have to live there,' Phoebe had said indignantly. 'Isn't it noisy and dirty and smelly for them?'

Jane had laughed. 'Dearest Phoebe, but those sort of people don't mind; they are used to it. And Reginald has been very generous and built a lot more houses, so almost every family that works in the mills can have their own. Some of the houses actually have three rooms.'

More houses no doubt meant more rents, Phoebe thought. Reginald and Jane lived richly on the toil of these people. She'd ventured into the town one afternoon, and seen tiny ragged children, with bare legs and arms and no shoes even in winter. The older ones, she knew, worked in the mills. A few elderly, bent women had stood and watched her walk past, and Phoebe had shivered at the unconcealed enmity in their eyes.

'When do you leave us for your noble friends?' Dorothy, one of Reginald's sisters who lived with them, asked, when the two boys, still shrieking, had rushed from the room and they could resume normal conversation. 'We have never been invited to Ridgeway Park.'

'And whenever dear Reggie invites them

here they always decline, saying Lord Drayton is too frail to drive so far,' Hermione, the other sister, complained.

The sisters, aged twenty-five and twenty-six, were so alike they were often taken for twins. Small, thin, with pale crimped hair teased into ringlets which hung either side of their faces, they always wore a profusion of mainly ugly jewellery, and their gowns were laden with frills and bows and other garnishes. They wore perpetually disgruntled expressions which changed to cringing simpers whenever an unmarried man appeared at the house.

Reginald, unlike them, was large in every way. Tall, broad, with bulging muscles, he looked, Dr Kingston had said when he and Jane became betrothed, more like a prize fighter than a gentleman. 'But if he's what Jane wants, and after all she's never had another offer, I'll not refuse my consent.'

Phoebe, who had overheard these comments not meant for her ears, had wondered how Jane could possibly endure the sight of him for the rest of her life. He had an unusually large head, made even bigger by his mop of unruly black curls. His face was bland and round, his nose large and prominent, and his wide, thin-lipped mouth concealed big discoloured teeth. He had not changed a great deal in the thirteen years he had been married, except that his hair showed streaks of grey, and he had a grid of frown lines on his forehead.

Somehow Phoebe endured their envious comments, pointing out that Lady Drayton was employing her, not treating her as a social equal. When a message came, a few days after Christmas, that Lady Drayton would be sending a carriage for her on the following day, she breathed a sigh of relief and went to pack her belongings.

As the letter had been addressed to Mrs Kingston, Phoebe only heard the rest of the contents when she went back downstairs. Dorothy and Hermione were deep in a discussion of evening gowns.

'We can't both wear white,' Dorothy said. 'Why can't you wear the pale blue?'

'That old thing! It's last year's. I do think they could have given us more warning, so that we could have bought new ones.'

'They probably want to make us feel out of place, unsophisticated,' Dorothy said. 'They won't succeed. If you refuse to wear the blue, we could add different coloured trimmings to our white gowns. I'll have pink, you can have blue. Jane will lend us her maid to help us sew them on, and Phoebe, you'll have to help too.'

'What do you need them for?' Phoebe asked.

Dorothy smirked. 'Your noble friends have realized we are people of consequence, and have invited us to accompany you to Ridgeway Park for two days, to attend their dance for the New Year.'

2

'How plain everything is!' Hermione whispered, as a maid led them up the stairs to their bedrooms. 'There were only a few ornaments in the drawing-room, and just one picture on each wall. Do you think they are very poor?'

Dorothy giggled. 'They may have sold off everything else. I wonder if Lady Drayton's jewels are real or paste? Perhaps she had to sell them too. Jane said she had some lovely ones.'

Phoebe considered the Draytons had good taste, but did not comment. It would only provoke the sisters into making more disparaging comments on her own inferiority. She had been dismayed to hear the sisters were to attend the Draytons' ball, but Mrs Kingston had told her they always held a big party at New Year, and invited not only the important local families, but also their tenant farmers with their older children. Dorothy and Hermione would not like that, she thought with a grin. They enjoyed taking offence, and would probably conclude they were regarded as on the same social level as tenant farmers.

'They have never invited Jane,' Mrs Kingston said with a slight sigh. 'Beatrice told me once that it was too far for them to drive back afterwards, and she did not have enough rooms to offer them accommodation for the night. It's only because of you she has invited the girls.'

And still had not invited Jane and Reginald, Phoebe noted, and really could not blame Lady Drayton for not wishing to endure the company of her overbearing brother-in-law. Besides, once he had visited Ridgeway Park she would never be free of invitations to visit his home, and his attempts to advance the connection.

The sisters, having been shown to a large room they were to share, and Phoebe to a small connecting one, were complaining bitterly as soon as the maid left them.

'Why should she expect us to share, and not you?' Dorothy demanded, opening the connecting door and surveying Phoebe's room.

'Your room is three times the size of mine,' Phoebe said, irritated. 'Who would you expect me to share with? You are sisters. Have you never had to share a room before?'

'Only when we were little. Phoebe, you're Lady Beatrice's pet, can't you tell her you think her housekeeper, or whoever is responsible, has made a mistake? We need rooms to ourselves.'

'I would not be so rude! Besides, I imagine the house is full with all the guests they have staying. There might be a couple of attics, I suppose, unless they are occupied by all the visiting maids. Now please let me unpack what I need for dinner tonight. And I thought you still had some more ribbons to sew on to your ball gowns for tomorrow?'

She almost pushed them back into their bedroom, locked the connecting door, and undid her trunk. She had given up wearing white when she had her twenty-first birthday two years ago, considering it too juvenile. The one good evening dress she possessed was a delicate shade of primrose satin embroidered on the bodice and edge of the skirt in a deeper shade of gold, and her ball gown, saved from the days when she had attended balls in the Assembly Rooms, was of blue silk with a silver gauze overskirt. She took them out, shook them to get rid of the worst wrinkles, and hung them up, hoping the rest of the creases would drop out before she needed to wear them. She had no maid to press them, and Lady Drayton's maids would no doubt be far too busy to help.

It was almost time to dress for dinner. Phoebe washed, blessing the maid who had appeared with pitchers of hot water. She brushed her hair and bundled it into a net at the nape of her neck. Aware that if she did not escape, the sisters would demand her help with their own elaborate hairstyles, and complain when she was unable to make their intransigent curls behave as they wished, she slipped into the evening gown, threw a paisley shawl her mother had given her over her shoulders, and left the room.

Downstairs she found several of the guests already in the drawing-room. When she went in, Beatrice, wearing a narrow-skirted gown of sea-green silk, shot through with silver thread, came across to her, took her hand, and led her to meet two other young ladies, daughters of her older sister who lived in Lancashire.

Ten minutes later, Dorothy and Hermione appeared, followed by a tall, dark man. Phoebe shut her eyes and hoped no one knew she was connected to the pair. They looked more alike than ever, as they had both donned elaborate evening gowns of puce silk, adorned with ruffles of pink satin and dyed feathers in varying shades of pink. It looked, Phoebe thought, as she stifled a giggle, as though the dye had been uneven. Dorothy sported a magnificent diamond necklace which belonged to Jane, a wedding present from Reginald, while Hermione wore one of rubies which clashed horribly with her gown. Had they tossed to see which one wore the diamonds, she wondered?

As they entered the room through the double doors they separated to permit the man following them to step between them. He was tall, impeccably dressed in a black tail coat and white waistcoat, and the new fashion trousers. His cravat was tied in some vastly intricate style, and Phoebe idly wondered just what name was given to it. Identical simpers were cast in his direction by the sisters, and Phoebe stifled another giggle, this time at the harassed expression on his handsome face. He looked towards Beatrice, and she went across to them, drawing the sisters away and introducing them to Lord Drayton. The man visibly heaved a sigh of relief, and crossed the room to join Phoebe's group.

'Poor Uncle Zach!' the elder of the girls sitting with Phoebe mocked. 'You really do need to get married so that you are protected from predatory females.'

He grinned at her. 'Thank you, Priscilla, I have enough trouble avoiding all the girls your Aunt Beatrice thrusts under my nose without you adding your efforts. How are you both? I only arrived an hour ago, and haven't seen anyone yet.'

He turned to Phoebe. 'I'm Beatrice's brother, Zachary Walton.'

'Phoebe Kingston.'

So this was the man who would be escorting them to Brussels. Phoebe studied him with interest. He was, she judged, about thirty years old, and carried himself with military bearing. She wondered why he was not in the army. Conventionally handsome with short dark hair, a thin face, and brilliant blue eyes, he would attract attention and admiration wherever he was. From the remarks of his nieces, she understood he attracted plenty of female attention and was not surprised. Dorothy and Hermione had quite clearly admired him. Phoebe didn't know them well, but during the Christmas festivities at Bradshaw Towers she had concluded that they attempted to flirt with any unattached man under sixty.

It was difficult, she knew, with a pang of remorse for her uncharitable thoughts, for girls who wished to marry to do a great deal about it. Daughters of the upper classes were introduced to Society, where they might meet suitable husbands. Many marriages were still arranged by the parents, to consolidate estates, or increase the influence of families. Girls like Dorothy and Hermione would normally marry men like their brother, mill owners or professional men such as doctors or lawyers. To marry into a higher class was rare, unless a girl was especially pretty or wealthy. To marry someone like a shopkeeper would be considered a step down in the social scale. For a few moments she felt sorry for Reginald's sisters. They were not pretty, and their manner was unfortunate. She doubted whether Reginald or Jane had made much effort to introduce his sisters to suitable men. Reginald would probably not have considered it, or if he had, might not have wanted to offer dowries. Jane probably found them too useful as helpers around the house to want to lose them. For a moment she wondered why Jane had not expected one of them to take over the task of teaching her children; then she concluded Reginald would most likely have objected. His sisters could not be used in such a fashion, but to let Jane's sister take on a menial role would not offend him.

Her musings were cut short as dinner was announced. She was seated between two young men, both sons of local squires, and in between talking to them was able to watch Dorothy and Hermione, seated on the far side of the table. Their table companions were older, and both men had wives present. This obviously displeased the girls, who kept casting resentful glances at Phoebe and the lively conversations she enjoyed with the young men.

When Beatrice led the ladies into the drawing-room Dorothy took Phoebe's arm and marched her across to a sopha in a far corner of the room.

'You were behaving disgracefully!' she hissed. 'You were flirting all through dinner. I felt thoroughly ashamed of you.'

Hermione had joined them and seated herself on Phoebe's other side. 'If Reginald hears about how you are letting him down he will not permit you to go on this silly Brussels jaunt.'

Phoebe laughed. 'Your brother has no authority over me, to allow me to go anywhere, and I shall talk to or flirt with — if that is how you choose to describe friendly conversation — whomsoever I like. At least I don't simper at men who are unlikely to appreciate such infantile behaviour!'

As they spluttered with indignation Phoebe rose to her feet and walked calmly across to where Priscilla and her sister were looking at a book of flower paintings. They welcomed her, moving to make room for her to sit beside them, and chatting until the men came in. Soon afterwards several card tables were organized, while some of the younger men went off to play billiards. Phoebe and her new friends went with them to watch. When one of the men who had been talking to Phoebe asked Dorothy and Hermione if they were coming, they quickly shook their heads.

'I am not interested in such ways of passing the time,' Dorothy said, and the friendly man shrugged and left them.

'They'll become sour old maids,' Priscilla said, and Phoebe knew she was right. There was nothing she could do to help, and their attitude towards her did not make her want to try and help them. When she went to bed she made sure the connecting door between their bedrooms was locked, resolutely ignoring the insistent rapping on it, and the demands for the door to be opened.

★   ★   ★

On the following day Phoebe rose early, as she usually did. It was a bright, sunny day, and she longed to be outside, away from the sisters who would, she was sure, spend the day being critical of their hosts and the other guests. The only other person in the breakfast-room was the Earl of Wrekin, dressed in immaculate buckskin breeches and high boots. He rose to his feet as she entered and offered to help her from the dishes set out on the sideboard.

'Thank you, my lord. Just a slice of ham please.'

He put the plate in front of her. 'You are up unusually early. I thought most ladies preferred to stay in bed for several more hours.'

'Oh? Ought I not to be here? Was I expected to stay in my room?' Phoebe asked, worried she had made a social gaffe.

'Don't be concerned. It is a pleasant change to see a girl who has energy in the mornings. What do you mean to do to fill the hours?'

'I thought I would walk in the grounds, unless it rains, but it looks as though it will be a fine day.'

'There is not a great deal to see in the gardens at this time of year, except bare trees and dead plants. Do you ride?'

'I used to, before my father died.' Phoebe thought wistfully of Rusty, the gentle mare they had been forced to sell when her father died, because they could not afford to keep her.

'Beatrice has a mild-mannered mare she would lend you, if you cared to come out for a ride with me.'

Phoebe's eyes lit up. 'Oh, that would be wonderful.' Then she remembered. 'But I don't have a riding habit with me.'

'I'll ask Beatrice's maid if she can find an old one.' He rang the bell as he spoke. 'My sister probably has several. Ah, Peters, can you please ask Lady Drayton's maid to find a riding habit and some boots for Miss Kingston? Then send to the stables to have her mare and another horse for me saddled.'

When the butler had left, Wrekin poured Phoebe some more coffee. 'You live in Yorkshire?' he asked.

'I do now, but we used to live in Buxton. My mother has been unwell, she and I have just come to make our home with my sister and her husband.'

He clearly did not know he was destined to escort her to Brussels. No doubt Beatrice would tell him. If he knew she was a mere employee, would he be willing to ride out with her? Just in case he was not, she would not mention it herself. The opportunity to ride out for the first time in over four years, since they had been forced to sell her horse, was too precious to jeopardize.

Peters reappeared, saying her ladyship's maid would meet the young lady in her bedroom. Phoebe swallowed the last of her coffee, jumped up, and almost ran from the room. Within a quarter of an hour she was walking into the stable yard, the skirt of a very elegant dark-green habit looped over her arm, and a matching military-style hat perched on her head.

Two horses were waiting, a tall, rangy chestnut gelding and a smaller, dainty black mare. The earl was talking to a groom, but he turned when he heard Phoebe's footsteps and smiled at her.

'Good, you don't waste time. Let's go.'

★ ★ ★

Phoebe did not see Dorothy or Hermione until it was time for dinner before the ball. She and the earl had ridden up on to the moors, and when he saw she was a confident rider he led the way along an ancient track which was an old drove road, letting the horses stretch their legs in an exhilarating gallop.

He had brought food, and they had picnicked under an ancient oak tree, talking about the scenery. The earl told her about his own home in Shropshire, beside the River Severn, much gentler country, and Phoebe spoke of her life in Buxton. She did not like to mention Brussels. He might think she was being too forward. It was the middle of the afternoon before they returned to the house.

'You will ache,' he said, as he lifted her down from the saddle. 'Soak in a bath or you will be unable to dance tonight. I warn you, I shall ask you for a waltz, and I cannot tolerate partners who plead soreness or exhaustion.'

Phoebe had taken his advice, and the maid looking after her lit the fire in her bedroom, brought a hip bath and a procession of footmen carrying cans of hot water, and stayed to help Phoebe wash her hair. As Phoebe sank into the scented water she sighed with pleasure. This was so different from their genteel poverty in Buxton, and the grudging provision of just three extra cans of hot water once a week, which was all Jane permitted in the way of a bath.

Kneeling in front of the fire rubbing her hair dry, Phoebe recalled every moment of the day. In the earl's company she had not thought of the moors as bleak and inhospitable. He had talked about the birds they saw, pointed out a couple of deer hiding behind some straggling bushes, and said he loved coming here when the heather was in flower. She would enjoy travelling to Brussels in his company, she decided. If she had had any qualms about this first journey so far away from home, she no longer felt them.

There were fewer people sitting down for dinner tonight, just the house party. Phoebe had contrived to avoid Reginald's sisters during the rest of the afternoon, and in the drawing-room before dinner she had talked to Priscilla and the earl, giving them no opportunity to reproach her for perceived faults, though both of them had glowered at her in a manner which promised they would have plenty to say later. Hermione joined the small group and, simpering up at his lordship, began to relate all they had done during the day. It seemed mainly to consist of viewing the pictures of Lord Drayton's ancestors in the picture gallery, helping Lady Drayton arrange flowers, and resting in their room in preparation for the evening's exertions.

'So where were you all day?' she asked Phoebe, her tone hardening.

'I took Miss Kingston riding,' the earl replied for her.

Hermione gasped. 'I hope you took a groom! It's not at all the thing for an unmarried girl to ride out with a man she's not related to.'

The earl looked down at her, his glance haughty. 'Are you implying that Miss Kingston would not be safe in my company?' he asked, his voice silky.

Hermione, flustered, lost herself in a maze of denials, apologies and excuses.

Priscilla eyed her with interest. 'You need not be concerned for Phoebe's virtue,' she said. 'Uncle Zach is determined not to marry, so he's not going to compromise any girl and fall into parson's mousetrap.'

Hermione, flushing unbecomingly, retreated to where Dorothy was sitting with one of the older ladies. The earl, trying to look stern, chastised his niece for her language and her forward behaviour, and then had to leave them to take his dinner partner into the dining-room. Priscilla merely chuckled.

'She probably wished he'd taken her out. It would have done her no good. He only flirts with married ladies,' she whispered to Phoebe, 'but he'll have to marry in the end if he doesn't want our great-uncle Jonas and his horrible brat to inherit,' she added with a grimace.

There was no time for more, and Phoebe was left wondering what was the matter with Jonas and his son that made Priscilla dislike them.

The guests for the ball began to arrive as soon as dinner was over. Phoebe had not seen the ballroom before, which was attached to one side of the house, but when she went in she gasped in delight. It looked like a magic winter fairyland. Greenery, fir trees and swags of holly and ivy were all around the room, arranged to create small alcoves which could be used for those who were not dancing. Lit by several chandeliers, the candles reflected a hundred times in the crystal drops and glittered on something which had been used to make it appear the trees and leaves were covered with frost.

The earl was dancing with his sister's younger guests, but Phoebe had no shortage of partners. Occasionally one of the older men invited Dorothy or Hermione to dance, but most of the younger men avoided them. They really did look most peculiar, in white satin gowns trimmed with pale-pink rose-buds and embroidered with dark-green branches and leaves across the bodices and round the hems. Dorothy carried a pale-pink shawl, Hermione a pale-green one. The dresses were far too young for them, almost as though they were in fancy dress, and their discontented expressions were not encouraging.

It was after supper, when Phoebe was wondering a little disconsolately if the earl had forgotten he had said he'd dance with her, when he appeared at her side. She saw Dorothy glaring as he led her on to the floor. No doubt the report that went back to Bradshaw Towers would be critical and accuse her of being fast. She determined she must write to her mother and give her own account before those cats prejudiced Mrs

Kingston and gave her a false impression of her behaviour. She did not think Mama would believe bad rumours about her, or change her mind and not permit her to go to Brussels, but she suspected that if the sisters could spoil her chances they would do so.

'Not too stiff?' the earl asked as he put his arm about Phoebe's waist and swirled her into the crowd of dancers. It was a waltz, a dance she and some girl friends had learned just before Papa died, when it was considered so daring very few hostesses allowed it at their dances. She had never danced it in public, but to her relief the steps and the rhythm had not been forgotten.

'No,' she managed, but was too breathless, both at his closeness and the speed of the twirling, to say more.

'My sister tells me the Bradshaw sisters are your cousins.'

'No they are not!' Phoebe replied, horror-struck. 'They are not related to me at all. My older sister is married to their brother, that is all. It was very kind of Lady Drayton to invite them here,' she added, aware that she had sounded ungrateful.

He looked at her quizzically. 'They don't appear to be enjoying the experience. Do they go out into society much at home?'

'I don't think so. Reginald is a mill owner,

and though he would like to think of himself as a gentleman, I believe his social contacts are only with other businessmen. Oh dear, that sounds odiously top-lofty!'

He laughed. 'Refreshingly candid. Enough of them. You used to live in Buxton, you told me this morning. Was society there lively?'

'Until my father died four years ago, yes. I went to balls and the assemblies, and we had a host of friends. But since then we have led very quiet lives.' Of necessity, given our low income, she thought, and for the first time allowed herself to regret the lost opportunities, as well as the loss of her much-loved father.

He began to talk of other things, and all too soon the waltz ended. Phoebe had become used to the feel of his arm about her waist, and stepped away from him reluctantly as the music ceased.

'I'll say farewell now, I leave early in the morning for London,' he told her, as he escorted her to where she had been sitting with his nieces.

Phoebe felt a sudden sense of loss, then admonished herself. She would soon see him again, but she must take care not to read too much into polite conversation. He was attractive, but he treated all women in the same fashion. It meant nothing. He had not singled her out, or showed undue liking for her. He had taken her riding simply because she had been with him in the breakfast-room, and maybe he had taken pity on her.

★　★　★

Dorothy and Hermione departed, tight-lipped, the following day. Reginald had sent his own carriage for them, and Phoebe entrusted her letter to her mother to the footman accompanying it. Many of the other guests were departing also, and the air was full of farewells, thanks for the hospitality, and plans to meet again soon.

Beatrice sank into an armchair with a sigh of relief when the last of them had gone.

'Phoebe, let's have a cup of tea. I'm exhausted. I do enjoy entertaining, and as Lord Drayton rarely leaves home, apart from trips to Buxton to see his doctor or tailor, it is almost the only opportunity he gets to see his friends.'

When the tea tray had been brought and they were sipping the fragrant brew, she looked at Phoebe, a question in her eyes.

'Did your brother-in-law's sisters enjoy themselves? I'm afraid they did not appear to be having an enjoyable time.'

Phoebe looked straight at her. 'I don't

think they would enjoy anything if they were not the centre of attention,' she said. 'Please, you did everything you could to make their stay pleasant, except provide them with wealthy, handsome, titled husbands!'

Beatrice laughed. 'That would be beyond my powers, I fear.'

'But they are always dissatisfied. They cannot be very happy at home. Reginald is autocratic, and so much older than they are. And Jane, I'm afraid, likes to be in charge of everything.'

'I see. Phoebe, as soon as I return from escorting you to London I will ask your mother here for a long visit.'

Phoebe forced back a tear. How perceptive and kind she was. 'I think she would enjoy that. She loves Jane, of course, but she will be missing her friends in Buxton.'

'And you. How did you like Zachary?'

Phoebe blinked at the change of subject. 'I found him very pleasant. He was kind and took pity on me, I think, because I knew no one else here.'

'Zachary is well-mannered, polite, but I would not consider him a man who normally makes special efforts to entertain lonely girls. He enjoys feminine company but he is, I fear, an incorrigible flirt. My dear, don't allow yourself to feel a *tendre* for him.'

Phoebe flushed. 'Of course not! It would be

quite inappropriate. I'm your employee.'

Beatrice smiled but said no more about her brother. 'We'll spend a couple of days quietly, to recover, then we'll set off for London.'

★ ★ ★

On the following day Phoebe received a letter from her mother, brought over by Reginald's groom, who said he would wait for any reply. It was spotted with tearstains, and Phoebe opened it in some trepidation. Had the sisters persuaded her to withdraw permission to go to Brussels?

To her relief the letter was full of advice about how to behave, pleasure that she had enjoyed the ball, and repeated assurances that she was being well cared for by Jane and her servants.

I will miss you, naturally, as we have never before been apart, but I will look forward to your return.

Phoebe immediately sat down to reply, promising to return in a few months.

Sally will no doubt become betrothed to someone while she is in Brussels, she wrote, *and I will be free to come home.*

But not for long if she could help it, she added to herself, feeling guilty at abandoning her mother to Jane's ministrations. She comforted herself with the thought that her mother would understand. After all, if she had married, she would have left home. Surely, amongst all the people now flocking to Brussels, she might find another congenial position as companion? Especially if she had done the job with Sally successfully, and could expect a recommendation.

★ ★ ★

Benton Manor was a delightful house built in Tudor times. The walls were of glowing Cotswold stone, covered with creepers; the mullioned windows twinkled in the winter sunlight, and the many twisted chimneys rose high above the roof. Phoebe wondered just what improvements Lady Benton wanted to make. If the manor belonged to her she would not alter a single thing.

When the butler showed her and Beatrice into the small, panelled drawing-room they found Lady Benton looking at some drawings spread out on a large table. She looked up at them, frowning slightly, seeming distracted, then she smiled and came forward to clasp Lady Drayton's hands.

'My dear Beatrice, you are my saviour! I don't know what I would have done if Sally had been left to plague me for much longer.'

Beatrice pursed her lips. 'Surely she cannot be so dreadful? The chit's only just seventeen, barely out of the schoolroom.'

'Old enough to cause endless trouble.'

She turned to Phoebe, raising her eyebrows slightly. Beatrice introduced her. 'Phoebe looks young, but she is three and twenty, and a very sensible girl. It will be better for Sally to have someone nearer her own age as a companion; someone she can regard as a friend.'

'If you think so. But do come and look at what my architect, Nathaniel Cowper, has designed for me. I'm having the front completely remodelled in the classical style, and the walls of these dreadfully poky rooms taken down so that we can have more commodious reception rooms. But I don't know if this portico is large enough. Look at this drawing. It does not look the right proportions to me.'

'Later, Clara. Perhaps we can be shown our rooms? I'm sure Phoebe wants a rest, and I most certainly do. It's been cold travelling.'

'Oh, forgive me! I'm so taken up with this

project I lose sight of everything else.'

Including her daughter's welfare, Phoebe thought, and wondered when she would meet the girl.

They were shown to two small rooms where large fires roared in the fireplaces. At least Lady Benton's housekeeper had prepared a welcome. Phoebe unpacked the valise she was using for overnight and changed into her one evening gown. Beatrice had said they would stay just two nights, and with an early start should reach London in a single day, if the weather held.

As she brushed her hair she looked out of the window. Despite the cold she had opened it slightly, for the fire was hot and the room stuffy. Below was a small knot garden, surrounded by a tall yew hedge. Phoebe assumed herbs were grown in the pleasant, sheltered spot. At this time of year the plants were straggly, some of the stalks bare, but in the summer it would be a charming sight. Then her attention was drawn to voices below her window, and she glanced down. A young man, scarcely more than a boy, was clasping a girl in his arms, and she appeared to be weeping bitterly. He stroked her hair, which was an unusual shade of red, and whispered into her ear.

Embarrassed at witnessing such a scene,

Phoebe drew back and gently pulled the casement closed. It was two of the servants, she assumed, perhaps a lovers' quarrel being resolved.

A little later she knocked on Lady Drayton's door and they went down to the drawing-room. Lady Benton was there, having changed into an evening gown of bronze silk, but otherwise, Phoebe judged, having taken few pains with her appearance. Tendrils of hair escaped from under her tiny lace cap; she wore no jewellery, and was still poring over her drawings. This time a tall, thin man was with her, and he was gesticulating with quick, vehement movements.

Lady Benton looked up, smiled, and came across to them. 'This is Mr Cowper, my very clever architect, who is making such wonderful changes to the manor,' she said. 'Now I wonder where Sally is? I haven't seen her since this morning. Nor your nephew,' she added, her voice becoming hard.

'George is at the lodge, my lady, with the drawings, making the changes we agreed yesterday for the east wing. I left him there as he wanted to finish while it was fresh in his mind. He tends to become so absorbed he forgets the time, but he will be here soon, I'm sure.'

It was twenty minutes before a young man, looking rather flushed, entered the room and apologized for being late. On his heels came the most ravishingly pretty girl Phoebe had ever seen. She had a pale, flawless complexion, huge green eyes, luminous with unshed tears, and red hair which Phoebe had seen so very recently.

3

While they were at Benton Manor, Lady Drayton's butler, footman, her maid and an undercook went ahead to open up the town house, where normally only a caretaking couple lived, since the Draytons used it so infrequently. On the day after their arrival it was clear Lady Benton had no plans to entertain them herself. She told them at breakfast that Mr Cowper would be going to Northampton on the following day, to check on work his men were doing at a house there.

'So you see, I have to finish deciding on the work here today. But there are horses in the stables; you could ride out. Sally will show you the best rides. Where is the girl? Surely not still abed. Or you could take the carriage to do some shopping.'

'Phoebe might like to ride out, but I am weary of travelling, Clara, so I shall rest quietly, reading in the library, while you are with Mr Cowper.'

'You don't look well, my lady,' Phoebe said, when Lady Benton had left the room. 'You are very pale.'

'Just weary. But you must take the

opportunity of a ride. It's a beautiful day, and you've been confined for too long in the chaise.'

Phoebe could see she meant it, so she changed into the habit Beatrice had given her, and went to the stables. There she discovered from a harassed head groom that Sally had ridden out long before.

'I can't spare a groom to go with you; there's only me and Ted here, and he's got to do some errands for Lady Benton. But Poll here's steady as a rock, would carry a three-year-old safely. And ye can't lose the way, miss. Just beyond the gatehouse there be a track takes you to top of hill, and ye can see for miles there. Take track that goes behind the little wood of oak trees, and it comes out by home farm, and ye can see the manor from there. An hour's ride, if ye takes it steady.'

Phoebe thanked him, and mounted a stolid-looking dun mare. She preferred to be alone. She had a great deal to think about. It had, surely, been Sally she had seen the previous day in the little garden with the architect's nephew, and they had been embracing. Was this the sort of behaviour which made her mother declare she was a handful? Did Beatrice know? Was Sally, neglected as she seemed to be, in the throes of calf love? Would she forget the boy when she had other things to think about, such as new clothes and the excitement of being in London and then Brussels?

Most importantly, ought she to tell Lady Drayton? But despite her denials, Phoebe thought Beatrice was unwell. She ought not to bother her. Her indecisive thoughts occupied her until she reached the top of the hill and paused to look at the wintry scene. It was a bright, crisp day, and she could see for miles across the gently undulating landscape. Further to the west the Cotswold hills rose higher, bleaker and without the many woods and copses nearer to hand. Phoebe could see the church steeples and cottages of several villages. Smoke rose hazily from dozens of chimneys, and faintly she could hear the clang of a hammer on an anvil.

She turned eventually along the track leading to the oaks. As she neared them her stolid mare threw up her head and neighed, just as a couple of pheasants broke from cover at the edge of the wood and flew past the mare's head, less than three yards away.

Phoebe tightened her grip, then realized that Poll was not in the least disturbed by the birds, but had sensed the presence of some stable mates. Round the corner of the wood came two other horses, ridden by young men.

Phoebe recognized George Cowper first, and wondered how the architect's assistant was able to spare the time for riding out. Perhaps he had some errands to do for his uncle, though she could not immediately think of any likely ones. Then an exclamation from his companion drew Phoebe's attention, and she saw that instead of the youth she had at first thought, it was Sally, dressed in breeches and riding astride.

★ ★ ★

'Please don't tell Mama! She'd be horrified to know I ride in breeches.'

'And not that you have clandestine meetings with a man?' Phoebe demanded. 'I think you'd better come back with me.'

Phoebe, who had occasionally ridden astride when she was a child, had some sympathy. It was something she had often wished she could do now.

George had initially glared at her, then sulkily said they were doing nothing wrong. At a glance from Sally he had shrugged, turned his horse, and cantered away.

Sally had reluctantly turned back towards the manor and was riding beside Phoebe, volubly protesting.

'They're not clandestine meetings. You

make it sound disreputable, and it isn't. I've ridden out with George several times since he came here,' Sally said. 'There are no other young people in the district, and he often has little to do, for his uncle is one of those people who likes to control everything himself. Mama knows, and she doesn't mind, because there isn't always a groom to come with me. But we'll have to go to the gatehouse. I hate riding side saddle, so I leave my habit and side saddle there.'

Phoebe considered her. She was so young and obviously neglected by her mother. Would it do more harm to report what had happened than to ignore it? Having once, when she was fifteen, conceived a romantic attachment to one of her father's young assistants, Phoebe knew how rapidly such an attachment could fade once the object of her admiration had gone on his way. With all the excitements in store, Sally would probably forget George Cowper within days. She had been wrong to permit him to kiss her, but it could cause more problems and unnecessary distress to tell her mother about this unsuitable attachment. It was more than likely the fault of the young man. He'd taken advantage of a lonely, neglected girl. Besides, and for everyone's sake she had to consider this, it would also spoil her own chances of becoming a friend to Sally, the job she had been hired for. If Sally felt she could not be trusted, she would be unlikely to pay heed to anything Phoebe said. She would keep a very close eye on the girl, Phoebe promised herself, to make sure nothing similar happened again.

'Do you promise not to do anything like this again if I keep your secrets?' she asked finally.

Sally beamed at her. 'I knew you wouldn't be stuffy about it! We'll have left the manor tomorrow, and I won't see George again. But don't you sometimes wish you could ride in breeches, with such freedom, instead of those hateful, clumsy habits and side saddles?'

Phoebe laughed. 'Yes, I do,' she admitted. 'I did ride astride when I was a child, occasionally, but that was in a private field, on a pony, without any saddles, when we stayed with some cousins.'

'I was so afraid you would be ancient, like a really stern governess,' Sally confided, as they rode towards the gatehouse. 'I was dreading the journey, and being stuck in Brussels with no one I knew, but now I know it will be fun with you. We're to stay in London and buy clothes first, Aunt Beatrice said, and I shall be so glad to get rid of these childish ones I'm made to wear. There won't be anyone in

Town at this time of year, but it's the first time I've been since I was about ten years old. Never mind, all the interesting people will be in Brussels.'

★ ★ ★

They arrived at the Drayton town house in Brook Street late in the afternoon of the following day, and Phoebe left the chaise with considerable relief. It had been cramped with four of them, and none of her companions had been inclined to conversation. Lady Drayton was feeling feverish, but insisted it was merely a cold and she was quite fit to travel. Annie, Sally's elderly maid who was to accompany her to Brussels, was grumpy and answered only in monosyllables when asked some question. Perhaps because of this, or regrets at leaving her home, Sally was unduly subdued during the journey. Phoebe wondered whether she was missing George Cowper, but Sally never referred to him, and Phoebe had to hope she would soon forget her infatuation.

'Would you not prefer to make your come out in London?' she had asked as they reached the outskirts.

Sally shrugged. 'I don't mind. There are plenty of people in Brussels this year, now

Napoleon is imprisoned on Elba, so it makes no difference. It might be more fun. Mama is only interested in getting me married so that she doesn't have to pay any more attention to me. I'm so glad Aunt Beatrice found you. It would have been odious if she'd foisted an old dragon to chaperon me. We'll have fun together.'

Phoebe wondered just what sort of fun she was envisioning. At least George Cowper would not be there. From remarks Beatrice had made before they reached Benton Manor she gathered Sally had caused problems by her wild behaviour. Precisely what sort of problems these were, apart from what she had discovered for herself, she had not been told. Sally had mentioned she had suffered several governesses, from which Phoebe deduced they had most of them given in their notice. From her reading and the comments of her mother's friends, Phoebe had understood it was rare for impecunious women forced to earn their livings as governesses to voluntarily relinquish positions, since it could be difficult to obtain another. And if they left suddenly or after a short time, they might not be given good references. Perhaps only desperate women would assume the task of teaching girls like Sally. Had she been rash to agree not to reveal what she had discovered?

Only time would tell.

The first few days in London were taken up with choosing materials and styles for all the dresses Sally insisted she would need. Beatrice, though looking pale and tired, exercised some tactful restraint when Sally wanted to have gowns far too elaborate and old for her and, to Phoebe's surprise, Sally listened to her and discarded the more unsuitable ones. Phoebe, whose wardrobe was scanty, since they had been forced to economize since her father's death, was delighted when Beatrice insisted she also needed a considerable number of gowns, and said that her maid, who had been sent to London ahead of her with a few more servants, was an expert needlewoman and would quickly make some of her less important dresses.

'You will be expected to accompany Sally to parties,' she said, 'and you must be appropriately dressed. Lady Benton gave me a sum of money specifically for your dresses, and it is ample, so you need not worry about it. I am to give you some more so that you can buy whatever else you need in Brussels.'

For several days, therefore, Phoebe and Sally indulged themselves, collecting extensive wardrobes and more trunks in which to transport them to Belgium. Sally was cheerful, looking forward to the parties she expected to attend, and Phoebe decided all was well.

When not having fittings, or shopping for shoes and fans and reticules, they persuaded Lady Drayton's coachman to drive them around London. Lady Drayton, still trying to rid herself of her cold, admitted to feeling tired, and was glad of the opportunities to rest.

Sally had been to London before but declared she could not remember much of it. To Phoebe, never having been, the whole experience was magical. She could have spent twice as long gazing at the tombs in Westminster Abbey, or exploring the wonders of the British Museum, but Sally grew impatient, called her a blue stocking, and demanded to visit more of the shops in Bond Street.

Phoebe didn't mind. It was all new, and all exciting. Sally was proving to be a lively, friendly companion, and Phoebe enjoyed her company. She was beginning to think this was the easiest job in the world, enjoyable too.

They had been in London for just over a week before the Earl of Wrekin appeared. He had, Beatrice explained, been occupied with his own estates since he left Ridgeway Park, and had a few matters to deal with in London before he would be ready to escort them to Brussels. This could take several more days, but as he was coming to dine that evening, they would discover what his plans were.

Phoebe felt unaccountably nervous as she dressed in one of her new gowns, a pretty pale-blue sarsenet trimmed with lace. Perhaps it was Sally's remark that Zachary had not wanted to escort her to Brussels, and was only doing it to please Beatrice. Or it may have been the thought of meeting him again. She could not banish from her mind the recollection of that waltz, the feel of his arm about her waist, the faint male scent of him.

'He's a high stickler, no fun at all,' Sally complained, as they returned from a shopping expedition. 'He's old, too; thirty, I suppose.'

He hadn't seemed old to Phoebe.

'He's stuffy,' Sally added.

When she descended to the drawing-room with Sally before dinner, and found him already sitting with his sister, Phoebe cast him an anxious glance.

'You know Sally, of course, and Phoebe,' Lady Drayton introduced them.

He nodded to Sally, and shook hands with Phoebe. Then he looked enquiringly at his sister. 'I hadn't expected to meet you here,

Miss Kingston. But where is Sally's chaperon? Is she not to join us this evening? I had hoped to meet her.'

Beatrice laughed. 'Phoebe is Sally's companion, Zachary.'

He stared at her for a moment, frowning. 'Phoebe? Miss Kingston? Beatrice, are you out of your mind? How can a chit like this, who is no older than Sally, possibly be her chaperon? It's ridiculous, and I refuse to become involved. Either you find someone older, more suitable and responsible, or I refuse to escort Sally to Brussels.'

★   ★   ★

Phoebe felt as though she had been punched in the stomach. So this was the end of her dreams, the end of her attempt to escape from the stultifying atmosphere at Jane's house. Was she to be sent home in disgrace, a failure before she had even started on her job? Then she experienced a wave of fury and decided she was not giving in so meekly. She flung up her head and glared at the earl.

'I am three and twenty, my lord, and that makes me six years older than Sally. I have been accustomed to keeping house for my mother for four years, and controlling her finances. I'm no green girl.'

64

He frowned. 'Being able to deal with figures and do the marketing does not make you a suitable chaperon, Miss Kingston.'

Phoebe gasped. 'I did rather more than that, sir!'

He went on, ignoring her interruption, 'My sister tells me you have never even been to London before. How do you expect to go on in the sort of cosmopolitan society presently in Brussels? What authority can you exercise over a girl your own age? All right,' he added, as Phoebe opened her mouth to protest, 'a mere six years older.'

'I think I might have more influence,' she stressed the word and tossed her head, 'with Sally just because I am nearer to her in age and better able to understand her than an elderly spinster would!'

'I wouldn't dream of imposing a spinster, elderly or otherwise, on my niece. I expected, and I am going to insist on having, a mature, sensible woman who was or had been married and knows her way around. Beatrice,' he went on, swinging round to face his sister, 'how could you be so imprudent?'

Beatrice looked far too unwell to deal with this, but she made a spirited reply. 'Zachary, don't be tedious. I have known Phoebe for years, and she is a sensible, intelligent girl who has dealt with a great deal of responsibility since her father's death. I think I might be permitted to know what will suit a girl like Sally better than you, a bachelor.'

'And I don't want anyone else!' Sally said. 'I like Phoebe, and I promise I'll obey her when we get to Brussels. I'd hate to have a stuffy, old embittered widow spoiling everything I want to do, and if you force one on me I'll — I'll behave so outrageously you'll be sorry!'

Phoebe looked gratefully at her two supporters, struggling to suppress a grin at Sally's threats. Before she could speak, Lady Drayton, holding a hand to her head, spoke.

'Let us all calm down, and talk about this after dinner, which must be ready by now.'

Promptly, as though he had been listening outside the door, her butler came in and announced, with great solemnity, that dinner was served. The earl, compressing his lips and frowning, offered his arm to Beatrice, and left the room. As they followed, Sally grinned at Phoebe and leant towards her.

'Don't be concerned. Aunt Beatrice will change his mind, you'll see.'

★ ★ ★

The earl looked at his sister with concern. She had eaten almost nothing, pushing away untasted what he knew were some of her favourite dishes. She was flushed, and he wondered whether the argument before dinner had really offended her. It was unlike Beatrice to get upset over trifles. But then, it was unlike her to make such rash decisions as this choice of a chaperon for Sally. Later, when he could talk to her alone, he would be able to put his point of view without those two chits interrupting.

He accepted that it must have been a blow to Phoebe, expecting to go to Brussels and be involved in all the gaiety there. He would, of course, when he sent her back to her home, give her a sum to compensate for the salary she was expecting. And surely she could soon obtain another position. Being a companion to an elderly lady would be a far more suitable occupation than chaperon to his sister's wilful niece.

Phoebe was taking it well, he had to admit. She was smiling, talking quietly to Sally about the places they had been to during the past week, and ignoring the sullen responses. She avoided looking at him, however, and he felt a sudden twinge of remorse. He had enjoyed her company in Yorkshire, where she had seemed a sensible, well-educated girl, open and straightforward, employing none of the usual feminine tricks towards him, tricks which irritated him intensely. He admitted to himself he would have enjoyed more of her company, but she was quite unsuitable as a chaperon, and he wondered briefly if his sister had been subject to a mental aberration.

When Beatrice rose to leave the dining-room, Zachary held open the door for the ladies, while the butler placed a decanter of port on the table for him. Beatrice gave him a weary look as she passed. Sally glared at him and muttered something uncomplimentary under her breath. Phoebe, her head held high, walked past quickly without glancing in his direction, but he frowned when he realized she was holding her skirts to one side, as though fearing contamination should they come into contact with him.

He downed one glass of port swiftly, and poured a second. Tilting his chair he sipped at this, wondering whether there were any suitable women amongst his acquaintance who might be induced to chaperon Sally. No one came immediately to mind. If they were married they would be unable to leave their husbands and families. The widows he knew were mostly occupied with their children, and in a few cases, supervising the running of the estates left to them. One or two middle-aged spinsters, such as the sisters of an indigent peer whose land marched with his, living in straitened circumstances, might have welcomed the opportunity, as well as the salary, of a respectable occupation which enabled them to mingle with the *ton*. There was one ancient aunt, living alone in Kensington, but he doubted his ability to persuade her to leave her fireside and her cats during the winter. He regretted his impetuous words earlier, and wondered whether he might with dignity change his mind about not employing a spinster.

Setting down his almost full glass he decided to confront the ladies at once. As he went slowly up the stairs to the drawing-room, the door opened suddenly and Phoebe ran out. She didn't see him, but ran swiftly up the next flight, holding up her skirts and revealing shapely ankles.

What the devil had got into the girl, he wondered irritably? She had not, in Yorkshire, struck him as hysterical or prone to tantrums, but it looked as though the prospect of not being permitted to go to Brussels had finally overset her, however stoical she had appeared during dinner.

Shrugging, he went on into the drawing-room, to find his sister laid prone on a sopha, Sally fanning her with a copy of *The Ladies' Magazine*, and Annie standing behind the sopha wringing her hands and burbling something about burnt feathers.

'Beatrice! What's happened?' he demanded, striding across to her.

'She fainted, and it's all your fault for being so obnoxious!' Sally said. 'Couldn't you see she isn't well, and not in a condition to bear your bullying?'

At that moment Phoebe came back into the room.

'My lord, please stand back, she needs air,' she said briskly, pushing Sally gently out of the way as she knelt beside Beatrice. She held a small bottle under the lady's nose, and whatever it was seemed effective, for his sister opened her eyes and grimaced at the smell.

'Oh, do take it away,' she said faintly. 'I hate the stuff and will be quite well in a moment.'

'You have been unwell for days,' Phoebe retorted. 'You are in no fit state for arguments or decisions; you need to be in bed and not having to worry about anything.'

She rose to her feet and glanced at the earl.

'My lord, can you carry her ladyship up to her room?'

About to suggest it might be better to call two of the servants, he encountered Phoebe's look of doubtful enquiry, and stepped forward to scoop his sister into his arms, ignoring her protests that she was quite capable of walking.

'Nevertheless I mean to carry you. Beatrice, I hadn't realized you were so ill. You should have stayed in bed today.'

Phoebe had squeezed past him and when he arrived in his sister's bedroom she had the covers turned back, Annie was busy with a warming pan, and Beatrice's maid was warming a nightdress in front of a cheerful fire.

'Thank you, my lord, you can leave her to us now,' Phoebe said briskly, and the earl, somewhat to his surprise, found himself pushed out of the bedroom and the door closed with a snap behind him.

★ ★ ★

Lady Beatrice grew worse during the next few days, and Phoebe spent most of her time nursing her. The doctor forbade visitors, and Lady Drayton tried to insist that Phoebe and Sally kept away from her, for fear of infection. Phoebe ignored these commands.

'I looked after my mother through far worse,' she said. 'Your maid cannot do it all by herself, and you refuse to hire a nurse.'

'I much prefer familiar faces around me when I am feeling ill,' Beatrice said. 'I already feel better with your care. What is Sally

71

doing? How is she occupying herself?'

Phoebe laughed. 'Your brother takes her out driving or riding sometimes, and she and Annie appear to spend every morning shopping. She has discovered a source of cheap muslin and ribbons, and has had to buy another trunk to accommodate all her recent purchases.'

'As soon as I am a little better you must set off for Brussels. I expect Zachary is fretting to be there.'

'He says he still has work to do in London,' Phoebe told her, wondering if it was true, or if the earl was attempting to find some more suitable chaperon in her place. He had said no more to her, and Sally reported that the subject was never raised when she went out with him.

A few days later Lady Drayton was sufficiently improved to sit out of bed for a few hours each morning. Phoebe was helping her to settle, wrapping shawls round her shoulders and a rug over her knees, placing cordial and a book on a table beside her, and a firescreen to keep the heat of the fire from her face, when there was a frantic hammering on the door of her bedroom.

The maid had gone downstairs to fetch a hot tisane, so with a murmured excuse Phoebe went to open the door. Annie stood outside and, seeing how agitated she was, Phoebe stepped out into the corridor and closed the door behind her.

'Annie, what in the world is it? Is Miss Sally ill?'

Annie shook her head, tried to speak, and then with trembling hands held out a folded sheet of paper.

'It's for her ladyship,' she whispered, 'but I don't rightly know what to do with it, when her ladyship's not well. It might be upsetting if it's what I think that little madam's been and done.'

Phoebe took it from her, broke the wafer sealing it, and began to read.

Dear Aunt Beatrice

I'm sorry, but I can't go to Brussels. I know Mama arranged it because she doesn't want to have to concern herself with me and my come out, and she is hoping I will find someone there to marry, so that she doesn't have to give me a Season.

It would all be a waste of time, as I have already chosen the man I want to marry. I know you and everyone else will despise him, say I am marrying beneath me, but I don't care a scrap for that. I love George, and by the time you receive this letter we will be on our way to Scotland. Ready for when we come back, please can you send my clothes — my trousseau — to the Gatehouse at Benton Manor, where we will be making our home until George's talents as an architect are recognized.

Please thank Phoebe for all she did. She was fun to be with, and I hope she is not too disappointed to be missing Brussels.

Your loving niece
Sally.

Phoebe looked up at Annie. 'When did you find this?'

'Just now, Miss Phoebe, when I took in her chocolate. She went to bed early last night, and told me she was tired and I wasn't to wake her till after ten this morning. Why, the deceitful little baggage! Begging your pardon, miss, I shouldn't be talking about my betters that way, but how she could do this I don't know! She's gone off with that Cowper fellow, hasn't she?'

'Yes, but we ought not to let the other servants know or there will be gossip all over London. If we can find her in time and bring her back all may be well. Has she taken many clothes? And do you think she had letters from him which might still be in her room?'

'I haven't looked; I came straight for you. I can't bother her ladyship, her being unwell.'

Phoebe was making rapid plans. 'Annie, tell everyone she has a fever and only you and I are to be admitted to her room. But Lady Drayton is not to know, it will only fret her. As soon as her maid comes back I will come to you. Go now and see if you can discover what clothes she has taken.'

Ten minutes later, stifling her feelings of revulsion at invading Sally's privacy, she was searching the small writing-desk in her room while Annie went through the clothes.

To her surprise, for she would have expected Sally to destroy any correspondence from George, she found a short letter.

To my precious darling

You make me so happy! I will have horses waiting in Grosvenor Square by eight on Tuesday evening, and as it is full moon we can ride all night to get away from London as soon as possible. If you are strong enough to ride on a few stages past Barnet, we'll be well on our way before they discover your absence.

I cannot wait to make you mine,
Your devoted chevalier
George

'Has she taken a riding habit?' Phoebe demanded, and Annie shook her head.

'No, they're here, even the new one she had made in London.'

'What about her breeches?'

'What breeches, Miss Phoebe?'

'Didn't you know that she sometimes rode out in a man's breeches?'

'Well, I never! The shameless little hussy!'

'Never mind that. Can you tell what she has taken?'

'Just a couple of day dresses and a shawl, and one pair of walking shoes. And a couple of shifts. Has she gone to Gretna Green, miss? Oh, she'll never be accepted by the best people ever again.'

'She will if I can get her back. Annie, I'm going to take this letter to Lord Wrekin, and no doubt he will set off after them. I shall go with him to give Sally countenance, if it's not too late to save the little fool. But people mustn't know I've gone. Can you tell everyone I have a fever too? Fortunately I don't have a maid of my own, so you can say I've asked you to look after me as well as Sally. I could even come and sleep on the truckle bed in this room to make things easier for you, and no one is to be admitted for fear of spreading the infection.'

Annie was nodding. 'I'll do it, Miss Phoebe. If anyone can save her, you and his lordship will.'

4

Annie distracted the footman in the hall so that Phoebe could slip out unseen. From the house in Brook Street it was only a few minutes' walk to the earl's house in Grosvenor Square, but it was raining slightly and by the time she reached there she was regretting not having brought an umbrella. As she hurried along she prayed that he would be at home, and not already out on the business Lady Drayton had said he was engaged on. It was not yet eleven, and Phoebe was aware that even outside the Season fashionable gentlemen, dining at their clubs and sitting up half the night playing cards, did not rise early. If he was not there should she follow him, to the City or wherever he had gone, or somehow acquire a horse and follow Sally herself?

She abandoned the latter notion as soon as she had formed it. She had little authority over Sally, and would not, even if she could catch her and the deplorable George, be able to insist on their returning to London. The Earl of Wrekin was her only hope.

To her great relief she saw him emerging

from his house as she turned the corner into the square. His tiger was holding the reins of his curricle, and the earl, with a nod of thanks, swung up into the vehicle. Phoebe began to run.

'My lord, wait!' she called, and he turned his head, frowning, as she came alongside. She clutched the side of the curricle and attempted to regain her breath.

'What the devil do you mean, making such a spectacle of yourself? How on earth my pea-brained sister ever considered you a proper person for Sally to know, let alone suitable as her chaperon, I will never discover.'

Phoebe had regained her breath. 'Please stop arguing,' she said, as she picked up her skirts and clambered up beside him. 'There isn't time, and I can explain as we go. The Great North Road, please, as fast as you can.'

To her frustration, he sat and stared at her. 'Have you gone mad?'

'Sally is eloping, with George Cowper,' Phoebe said between gritted teeth. 'Only you can catch her and save her. Oh, do get on, and I'll explain as we go.'

He seemed at last to sense the urgency in her voice, and gave the horses the office. 'Well?' he asked grimly, as he turned out of the square.

Giving a sigh of relief Phoebe explained, and at his curt request read out the two letters. 'They won't have got too far. They planned to ride all night, but it came on to rain, so without the moon they could not have ridden fast. And by this evening Sally will be so tired she will insist on spending the night at an inn. She isn't used to riding astride for so many hours at a time. We can catch them before this evening.'

'Astride? Are you telling me the unprincipled chit is dressed as a boy?'

'She must be, as none of her riding habits is missing, and the letter says they will ride.'

He swore under his breath, some uncomplimentary words which appeared to be directed at both his niece and her lover. 'Very well, I will give chase. But I wish you had given me just a few minutes to prepare.'

'To pack a few clean shirts and cravats, and take up your valet?' Phoebe asked. 'What do they matter when Sally's whole future is at stake? We have to catch them before it's too late.'

'No, Miss Impudence, to collect an extra cloak for Sally to wear, and enough blunt for hiring new horses. I'll have to hope this pair can hold out.'

'I brought the money we've been given for shopping,' Phoebe told him. 'As for cloaks,

Sally has her riding cloak. We have to go quickly if we are to catch them before it's too late.'

'We are not going to catch them, I am,' he responded swiftly. 'I will borrow your purse, but you will go back to reassure my sister that the pair of you have not been abducted.'

'You need not be concerned. She won't know. As far as Lady Drayton is aware both Sally and I are confined to our rooms with fevers, and only Sally's maid is allowed to attend us.'

He looked at her in some amusement, the first relaxing of his severity since she had met him. 'Are you always such a managing female?'

She ignored that. 'You are not related to Sally. It will be necessary for you to remain the night at an inn. If she has already been accepted as a boy, and the inn is full, she and George could well be expected to share your room, even your bed.'

'I'll take care of that eventuality.' He drew up at the side of the road. 'Now, Miss Kingston, I would be grateful for the loan of that purse. You can retain enough to hire a hackney back to Brook Street. I am grateful to you for trying to help Sally.'

Phoebe thrust her hand into her pocket and gripped the purse. 'I am coming with you, my lord. You can hardly drive Sally home in an open carriage, just the two of you. And you cannot let her ride in a chaise by herself. You need me.'

★   ★   ★

While the horses were toiling up Highgate Hill, Zachary was still asking himself why he had not insisted on putting Miss Kingston down and sending her back to Brook Street. His people would wonder where he was when he did not return that night. He was not in the habit of disappearing without informing them where he might be found and at what time he was expected back home. They might make things worse by sending out to ask where he was. Then this deplorable episode might become public knowledge and Sally's reputation would be ruined.

He was, unfortunately, compelled to endure her company. He glanced at her and discovered that despite the hood of the curricle being up, the rain was driving in, her pelisse was wet and she was shivering.

'There is a rug under the seat. For goodness' sake wrap it round you. I don't want a chaperon with a streaming cold on my hands as well as Sally.'

She flashed him a mischievous smile, and

he suddenly discovered how pretty she was. Even the strands of wet hair plastered to her forehead did not detract from the beauty of her piquant, heart-shaped face, widely-spaced eyes of a deep blue, and well-shaped, kissable lips.

He brought his thoughts back to more seemly matters. It would not do to be thinking along these lines of a girl his sister was proposing he escort to Brussels. He'd thought her attractive and sensible when they'd first met in Yorkshire, and younger than she said she was. She had, he conceded, behaved sensibly in bringing Sally's letters to him and ensuring that Beatrice was not worried about them, but that did not reconcile him to the notion of such a girl being a suitable chaperon, or companion, as Beatrice had insisted was to be her role, for Sally.

'You did not appear to be at all surprised at Sally's wearing breeches,' he said.

Phoebe, occupied with wrapping the rug round her, glanced up at him. 'I met her out riding with George Cowper when I stayed at Benton Manor.'

'And you did not see fit to tell her mother or my sister about this?'

'She promised to behave properly if I kept her confidence. I decided it was better for me to make friends than to start off with her resenting me.'

'Her promises do not appear to be reliable.'

'No, and I shall not believe her in future.'

He sighed deeply. 'Miss Kingston, although you have forced me to accept your help and company on this occasion, you need not imagine you have persuaded me to agree to taking you to Brussels. I still believe you are not a suitable chaperon for Sally.'

'It really isn't your business who is to be Sally's companion, is it?' she asked gently. 'She is not related to you.'

He glanced down at her, annoyed. 'So you have the claws of a cat, do you, as well as the obstinacy of a mule?'

She gurgled with laughter. 'What a picture that conjures up! Do I have the face of a cat or a mule?'

'You know perfectly well what I mean. But I can be stubborn too, Miss Kingston, and you would do well to remember that.'

'Oh, well, if you do not escort us, I am sure Lady Drayton can arrange something else. Having come this far she is not going to meekly give up and obey the commands of her younger brother, is she?'

The impertinence. 'I should not have to remind you that I am the head of her family.'

'Surely not? She has a husband.' Suddenly

Phoebe laughed. 'If brothers and sisters retained authority over their siblings even after they were married, I should never escape from my sister Jane!'

'Are you betrothed, Miss Kingston? If you are, I cannot applaud your fiancé's sense in being so complaisant over this jaunt to Brussels.'

She chuckled. 'You see? You believe a fiancé should already have more authority over me than my mother, who was quite happy with the notion of this jaunt, as you call it.'

He ground his teeth together, but did not pursue the question. Beatrice would tell him. If she was betrothed, he pitied the poor man. Perhaps he would not ask. It did not concern him, and he had no interest in knowing.

★　★　★

They had to change horses twice, and the second time they found traces of Sally and Cowper, who had hired fresh riding horses only an hour beforehand.

'They must stop soon,' Phoebe said. She was becoming worried. It was almost dark, still raining, and they had come much further than she had expected Sally to ride. 'Why would they need fresh horses now if they meant to spend the night nearby?'

'They would not wish to stay at a busy posting inn, where there was a chance of meeting someone they knew. Perhaps they want fresh horses so that they can set off early in the morning. We will ask at every inn we pass from now on.'

'Won't that delay us?'

'Better than risking not finding them.'

To Phoebe's relief making these enquiries took little time. The earl had asked for descriptions of the hired riding horses, and one was a grey, the other spotted. At every inn where they halted his tiger leapt nimbly from his perch and vanished into the stables. A quick look, a word with the ostler, and he would come back shaking his head. Then he came running out from the yard of a large posting inn.

'They was seen passin' no more'n ten minutes ago, guv,' he reported.

'Then they'll most likely be at the next inn.'

The next one they came to was a poor place, with an ancient painted sign swinging crookedly from a pole protruding from the wall over the entrance. Here the tiger was back within seconds, nodding vigorously. He took hold of the bridles of the earl's horses and asked if he should stable them.

'Yes, for the moment. If they have room we must stay the night.'

He helped Phoebe down. She was stiff from the long drive, and despite the rug, freezing cold from the rain which had not ceased all day.

'Thank you,' she said, almost falling against him as her cold feet gave way when she stepped from the curricle.

'Are you all right?'

He sounded concerned, but no doubt he did not wish to have to deal with an ailing female who had forced her company on him.

'I will be in a moment, thank you. My feet are so cold there is little feeling in them.'

'Then let us hope they have a good fire.' He took her arm. 'Come, we'll go in and confront the culprits.'

The inn had just one room, the door opening straight into it. It was low-ceilinged, with only one small window which let in almost no daylight. In any case, Phoebe reminded herself, it was dusk outside, and gloomy because of the rain. The only light, and Phoebe was relieved to see it, came from a huge fire roaring in the fireplace. A young boy was crouched to one side, turning the spit on which a haunch of venison and a couple of chickens were being roasted. Phoebe's mouth watered. They had halted only for a cup of coffee during one of the changes of horses, and carried away some slices of bread and hunks of cheese to eat as they drove.

It was a moment before her gaze penetrated the gloom of the rest of the room, and she saw Sally, still in her breeches, sitting on a settle the far side of the fireplace. George Cowper was sitting beside her.

★ ★ ★

Zachary almost laughed at the stupefied expression on Sally's face when she saw him. Beside her, the youth he assumed to be George Cowper shrank back into the settle, looking horrified.

'At last, my dear Sally. You have given us a long journey.'

'What are you doing here?' Sally croaked.

'I came to escort you back to London. And in the process, I will be preventing you from ruining your reputation and your life, my child.' He glanced round, just as the innkeeper, wiping his hands on a rag, came through a door which led, he assumed, to the kitchen quarters.

The innkeeper came forward, bowing obsequiously. 'Sir, Madam, I regret my two rooms are both taken,' he said, casting a jaundiced eye at Sally and George.

Zachary assumed they had bargained a

cheap rate for the rooms. 'Oh, don't be concerned, my good fellow. We will share with my young friends here.'

'I won't go! And you can't stay here,' Sally protested.

'Why not, child?'

Sally turned to George, who was still huddled on the settle. 'George, tell him we won't give up. He can't force me to go back.'

George swallowed hard. 'She's quite right sir. I don't know who the devil you are — '

'Beelzebub, perhaps,' Zachary put in softly.

'Who? Never heard of him. That's not to the point. Sally, that is Miss Benton and I, are betrothed and on our way to Scotland. You're not her brother or anything like that — '

'Certainly nothing like that, I'm thankful to say, but she is soon to be in my charge, and I do not wish to lose her!'

'You want to marry her for her dowry, I suppose!'

'I certainly do not wish to marry her, and I doubt if her dowry, however large, would make a great deal of difference to my own wealth. I am the Earl of Wrekin, since your betrothed does not see fit to introduce us.'

Cowper paled and looked rather sick. 'The Earl of Wrekin? Sir, I had no idea.'

'I thought you hadn't.'

Sally, seething with frustration, cut in.

'George, tell him he can't do anything! And — and if he tries to take me back by force, say you'll fight him!'

''Ere, this is a respectable inn, this is, and I won't 'ave no fisticuffs,' the innkeeper, who had been standing by the door and staring at them, said, starting forward. Then he noticed that the boy by the fire had ceased turning the spit, and was staring open-mouthed at Sally. He turned his anger on him, bidding him watch what he was doing, or they'd have meat burnt to a cinder one side and raw the other.

Behind him, Zachary heard a choke of laughter from Phoebe, and surveying the irate innkeeper, and George cowering on the settle he had difficulty in suppressing a smile.

'My apologies, Sally, but I neglected to bring my sword, or my duelling pistols. You can blame Miss Kingston for being in such a panic to follow you she gave me no time to pack essentials.'

'George, knock him down! You can do that, surely. You told me you were the champion pugilist at your school!'

'Sally, we can't start a brawl here. We must appeal to his lordship to be reasonable.'

'I will be very reasonable. If Sally comes back without any more histrionics I will not prosecute you for abduction of an heiress.'

'You wouldn't!' Sally was appalled.

'I would, Sally. Make no mistake.'

Sally gulped, and threw herself on to George's lap, weeping hysterically and swearing she would not go back to London.

To Zachary's relief Phoebe stepped forward. 'Leave her to me. Sally, let's go up to your room and talk quietly, away from these men who are only interested in fighting.'

★ ★ ★

An hour later Phoebe returned to the taproom. George, she was thankful to see, had gone, and the earl was seated by a table which had been laid for a meal. A buxom woman, whom she presumed was the innkeeper's wife, was busy setting out plates and knives. When Phoebe came in she bobbed a curtsy and retreated to the kitchen.

The earl rose to his feet, poured her a glass of wine and brought it across to her. 'Here, it's tolerable. Better than I would expect to find at such a place. Where is Sally?'

'Thank you. She is asleep. The poor child was exhausted and cannot face any food.' Phoebe sipped the wine gratefully. 'I need this. Where has that lovely meat vanished to? I could eat the whole of it.'

'It's being prepared in the kitchen,

proper-like for gentry, according to the innkeeper.'

'I hope they don't take too long. Where is the amorous swain?'

'He very soon saw the wisdom of departing and spending the night at another inn, on his way back to Benton Manor. I don't think he was relishing having to explain to his uncle, or whatever Clara's architect is, why he absented himself without permission.'

'Good. He deserves a thrashing, the young fool.' She chuckled. 'I think Sally's faith in him wavered when he refused to attack you. It will be even more damaged when she realizes you routed him without a fight.'

At that moment the innkeeper and his wife came in, bearing trays on which Phoebe was relieved to see both the venison and the chickens, and several side dishes which the woman proudly displayed. Finally, after being assured several times that they required nothing else, they withdrew, and Phoebe, glancing apologetically at the earl, picked up a bread roll and tore it apart.

'Forgive me, my lord, but if I don't eat soon I shall collapse,' she said, and nibbled at the bread while he carved slices of venison for her.

When they were finished, with the remnants of the meal cleared away, and a bottle of port placed on the table, the earl drew two chairs near to the fire. He poured two glasses of port and brought them across to Phoebe, handing one to her.

'I know port is not considered a drink for a lady,' he began.

'But I suspect you consider me no lady,' Phoebe said, taking the glass. 'After my father died, I developed quite a taste for it as Mama and I had to make do with the wine he had laid down. We didn't tell Reginald we had it, or he would have taken it to his own house, and we would not have been able to afford to buy wine. Papa was quite a connoisseur, I believe.'

'Reginald?'

Phoebe frowned. 'Reginald Bradshaw, my sister Jane's husband. He owns mills in Yorkshire, not far from Ridgeway Park.'

'Is that how Beatrice comes to know you?'

'No. My father was a doctor, in Buxton, and Lord Drayton used to consult him.'

'But I understood you were living with your sister.'

'Mama had been very ill, and we did not have much money. There were the medicines to buy. Jane persuaded Mama to live with her, and was expecting me to become an unpaid governess to her odiously undisciplined children. Lady Drayton took pity on me, and offered me the post as companion to Sally.'

Phoebe bit her lip. He might be unwilling to escort her to Brussels, but when Beatrice recovered, she was sure that lady would find some way of sending her and Sally there.

The earl was silent for a few moments. He rose to his feet and began to pace about the room. 'Is Sally reconciled to coming back to London?'

'Oh yes, she is now.'

'How did you persuade her?'

Phoebe grinned. 'I pointed out that anyone who really wanted to protect and marry her would not have allowed you to prevail with mere words, and if he really loved her he would not be deterred by a threat of prosecution. He would have answered you, found a way of rescuing her. And he would have provided her with a coach and four, not expected her to ride all the way to Scotland.'

'Are you always as devious?'

'Only when it proves to be necessary. Now, my lord, if you will excuse me, I really would like to retire.'

★　★　★

It was some time before Zachary himself went up to the tiny room under the thatch.

He was thankful to find a fire in the small fireplace, and that the bed had been properly warmed.

He hung up his coat as best he could, and resigned himself to having to wear the same shirt on the following day. He had not had to do that since he sold out from the army after his younger brother had been killed. At a more important inn, he reflected with a sigh, he could have expected someone would launder his shirt and cravat, and press his coat, but he suspected that the innkeeper and his wife, and the boy who had proved to be their son, were the only people running the inn, and they either had enough to do, or did not think it necessary to provide such refinements for their usual customers.

For the first time in his life, he thought, he would have to wear the same cravat for two days. He hoped none of his friends would see him as he drove back home.

In the morning Sally was subdued, replying to questions with no more than a yes or no. She had, Zachary was relieved to see, donned a gown. When he asked how she would explain to the innkeeper that she was not a boy, Phoebe intervened.

'We told them last night, of course. Otherwise how could we have shared a room? They'd heard enough to know what the situation was. But you need not be concerned: they don't know who we are.'

'They heard me tell Cowper who I was.'

'Oh, so they did. But don't be concerned. None of the Quality would ever stay here, so no one will know. If the landlord tells any of his cronies they will think he is romancing. And they don't know who Sally is, and that's what's important.'

Phoebe was as neat as ever, and he wondered how she contrived to have her gown, which had been wet and splashed with mud the previous day, looking so fresh. He was a little sorry that her hair was neatly brushed. When it had been wet and dishevelled the previous day it had made her, in some inexplicable way, look even prettier than she did now.

'We must squeeze into the curricle as far as the next posting inn,' he told them, dragging his mind back to practicalities. 'I will hire a chaise for the two of you, and we will travel together.'

Sally looked up and frowned. 'You'll act as a guard? To a prisoner? Don't you trust us?'

'I would describe it as escort, child, but if you choose to see me as a guard perhaps it will remind you of your folly. Can I trust you not to behave stupidly again?' he demanded.

'Sally will be all right with me. She knows

she has been thoughtless, and regrets the inconvenience she has caused.'

He regarded Phoebe steadily, then nodded. 'Sally, if you promise to behave yourself, I will withdraw my objections to Phoebe going to Brussels with you.'

5

The post chaise deposited them in Brook Street as dusk was falling, and the earl drew rein behind it. Sally, clutching Phoebe's hand, turned impulsively to him as he walked towards them.

'Please, can you distract the butler so that we can slip in without him seeing? Then no one else need know what I've done.'

Phoebe nodded towards him. 'It would be less worry for Lady Drayton,' she said.

After a slight pause he nodded. 'I will call tomorrow to talk to you.'

While she and Sally stood to one side he plied the knocker. As he disappeared into the house the two girls crept forwards. Phoebe opened the door, glanced into the hall and, seeing it empty, beckoned Sally. They fled up the stairs, trying not to giggle, and burst into Sally's room to find Annie sitting placidly beside the fire hemming handkerchiefs.

She rose to her feet, peering closely at Sally. 'So you're back. Is all well?' she added, glancing at Phoebe.

'Yes, we caught up with them late last night, so stayed at an inn. Young Mr Cowper has returned to Benton Manor,' Phoebe told her. 'How is Lady Drayton?'

'Much better, though she hasn't ventured from her room yet. It's been a really quiet house.'

'Were we missed at all?'

Annie chuckled. 'Not for a moment, though Cook is disappointed at your lack of appetites. I've kept back what food I could, so if you are hungry now there is some soup here in the saucepan, it won't take a minute to warm through, and rolls from breakfast.'

The breakfast provided by the inn had been meagre, and they had stopped on the road only for coffee. Phoebe and Sally ate hungrily.

'I think I had better be recovered tomorrow,' Phoebe said. 'Sally can wait another day or so, she was far worse than I.'

Sally pouted, but accepted Phoebe's decision. Saying she was still stiff from the long ride the previous day, she undressed and got into bed, while Phoebe went to her own room. She was weary too and, as soon as Annie had brought her supper, she undressed and lay in bed. It was impossible to sleep, though. They had averted disaster so narrowly. If they had not caught the runaways Sally's reputation would have been in tatters. She would never have been accepted in

Society again. Quite possibly her father would have disowned and disinherited her.

Would she be able to control Sally's starts in Brussels? She held no illusions that her situation as the girl's companion would be an easy one. Sally might be subdued now, and willing to promise anything, but she was young and lively. Her natural resilience would reassert itself, and who knew what sort of mischief she would think of next? If she had been really attached to the wretched George, anger and disappointment might make her careless of the opinions of others.

Phoebe's thoughts turned to the earl. After his first arrogance he had accepted her company and, she thought, even been thankful for her help with Sally. He had been kind and considerate for her comfort. Their conversation on the road had been mainly to do with the chase, but she had detected a sense of humour as well as command in his dealings with George and Sally. And, she thought with a smile of contentment, he had changed his mind about escorting her to Brussels. She would be going there with him, without the need for making different arrangements for their journey, as she had threatened Beatrice could do.

He was, she thought sleepily, very hand-some, elegant in his dress and competent in all he did. Lady Drayton had told her he had been with the army in the Peninsular, but she had not explained why he had left it to become a civilian and work for the Foreign Office. His dancing had been graceful, he rode well, his driving had been excellent, even when he had strange horses. She wondered why such a paragon, titled and rich, had not yet married. On the thought, she fell asleep.

★　★　★

Lady Drayton came downstairs for the first time the following day, Phoebe joined her in the drawing-room in the afternoon, feeling rather guilty that she had to conceal Sally's escapade. Sally herself had declared she meant to remain in bed for another day. Phoebe suspected she was sulking, angry at having her plans upset rather than regretting the loss of George. She would probably imagine herself in love many times over the next few years.

'Zachary was here this morning,' Beatrice told her. 'There is, unfortunately, more delay. He has to visit some elderly soldier who can brief him on conditions in Brussels, and the people he needs to meet there, but he means to start for Brussels a week today. We've been in London for longer than I expected, but it

100

has given you and Sally plenty of time to shop for suitable clothes. I confess I shall be glad to be back in Yorkshire, but as I don't feel strong enough to travel yet, a week's respite after my illness will be welcome.'

When Phoebe told Sally this the girl declared she wished to go shopping for a few more items she had not yet been able to find.

'I didn't bother overmuch before,' she admitted with a rueful grin, 'as I expected to be in Scotland with George, not on my way to Brussels. But if I have to go there, I mean to cut a dash.'

Phoebe merely blinked. She considered Sally had bought twice as much as she could possibly need. As for cutting a dash, she dreaded what Sally meant by this remark, but decided she did not want to know until it was time to take action.

They set off on the following morning, and Phoebe soon thought she understood what Sally had meant. They went first to a fashionable milliner, and Sally spent an hour trying on all the hats the lady could show her. Eventually she chose two, elaborate confections which were far too old for her.

'Are you sure?' Phoebe asked. 'They have so much trimming that they seem designed to draw attention from the wearer. I imagine elderly but vain ladies with raddled complexions would love these hats, hoping people would look at them rather than their faces.'

Sally gave her a startled glance, then considered the hats again. 'But I want people to look at me, not my hats.'

'No one would prefer to look at *Mademoiselle*'s hats instead of her pretty face,' the milliner said, regarding Phoebe with ill-concealed dislike.

Sally frowned. 'Perhaps the other one would be better,' she said, and Phoebe, suppressing a sigh of relief, handed her a simple hat adorned only with a feather dyed to match.

Having safely negotiated that obstacle, to the patently obvious annoyance of the milliner, Phoebe was wary when Sally said she wanted to go to one of the bazaars to choose some trimmings for her gowns.

'I know I have bought several, but I mean to be able to trim them with different ribbons, or lace, or gauze over-skirts, so that it seems as though I have a different gown each day.'

That seemed a harmless enough ambition, and Phoebe decided she would do the same herself. Not that she had nearly so many gowns as Sally, but it would be pleasant to be able to make them look different.

They were happily selecting ribbons when a girl a year or so older than Sally walking past shrieked with excitement and caught Sally's arm.

'Sally! I didn't know you were in London! What are you doing here? You must come and see me. Where are you staying?'

Sally swung round, laughed in delight, and kissed the other girl. 'Darling Emily! It's so long since I've seen you!' She turned to Phoebe. 'This is Emily Thorne, Phoebe. She's some sort of second cousin twice removed or something like that. Emily, Phoebe Kingston is my companion and going with me to Brussels to stay with my father.'

'Oh, you are lucky! I would dearly love to go to Brussels, but Papa won't hear of it.'

Phoebe smiled at Emily. She was excitable, but she and Sally seemed good friends. The two girls were soon chattering, and Emily said she would ask her mother to call on Lady Drayton that very afternoon.

'No one is in Town at this time of year, but we are having a small party in three days' time. Will you be allowed to come?'

'Of course, and Phoebe can be my chaperon if my aunt does not feel well enough. She has been ill.'

Emily's mother called that afternoon as her daughter had promised, and it was arranged.

Beatrice, still weak, was happy her charges would be entertained.

'For there has not been a great deal for you to do, I'm afraid, and I am unable to escort you.'

★　★　★

The elderly colonel Zachary had been sent to visit had fought his last battle over thirty-four years earlier, when, at Yorktown in Virginia, Lord Cornwallis with 7000 men, had surrendered to Washington, thus bringing to an end the War of American Independence. He had been badly injured, unable to rejoin the army, but he had, he told Zachary, followed every subsequent campaign with great interest, as well as all the political manoeuvrings.

'I know most of the men fighting today,' he boasted. 'I've followed their progress, and I think I can say I know their strengths and weaknesses.'

'I hope there will be no fighting in Brussels,' Zachary said, wondering what possible value these reminiscences could be to him. He himself knew the men who had been fighting in the Peninsular, before he had had to sell out.

'Humph! Don't believe it. Napoleon said

he'd be back with the violets, and he'll want to regain the Netherlands. He regards it as part of France.'

'But he's safely in Elba.'

'For now. There are plenty of people in Brussels and the rest of the Netherlands who would welcome him back. France is a good market for their goods. They lost many other markets when we blockaded their ports.'

'After all their suffering, and the thousands of young men who have been killed, do the people of France want him back, for all that to start again?'

The colonel shook his head. 'People can be odd. And it will depend, to some extent, on what is arranged at Vienna. If the Netherlanders approve, there will be no trouble. But you want to know about the men in Brussels.'

They spent the next few hours considering the people Zachary expected to meet, and he went back to London with his head full of facts and opinions. The old man, he decided, had been well worth a visit, even if his sometimes extreme comments were only partly true. At least now Zachary had a better understanding of the recent history of the Netherlands, and guidance on which men he might trust, and which to be wary of.

★ ★ ★

Phoebe was reading in the drawing-room on the following morning, alone because Beatrice and Sally had both chosen to breakfast in bed, and not yet appeared, when the butler came in, closing the door behind him carefully. He handed Phoebe a card.

'I told the gentleman I would ascertain whether you were in,' he said, and his voice was stiff with disapproval.

Phoebe, startled, looked at him in surprise, and took the card. What gentleman could wish to see her? And why did the butler seem reluctant to admit him. Then she gasped and understood. It was Reginald Bradshaw, and he never bothered to make himself pleasant to servants. But why was he here? He'd made no mention of plans to visit London. Was her mother ill? Or dead? She could not imagine any lesser disaster that would bring Reginald to London specially to see her.

'My brother-in-law,' she told the butler when she could speak. 'Please, show him up.'

She was pacing about the room when Reginald was shown in, but she went straight to him, ignoring the butler who was followed by a footman bearing a tray with a decanter of sherry and some ratafia.

'Mama?' she asked, her voice hoarse. 'Is she all right?'

'Of course she is. Why the devil should you

think otherwise? Jane's an excellent nurse, and the care she is receiving has already improved her health since she left Buxton and those dreadful lodgings you had. I came to ask when you remove to Brussels, and to see the earl.'

'He's not here,' Phoebe said, the relief at hearing her mother was well soon overcome by puzzlement at what Reginald wanted with the earl.

'Well, of course, I know he doesn't live here, but I don't have his direction. That was what I came to find.'

'He's gone out of London for a few days.'

Reginald heaved a deep sigh. 'How aggravating. When do you go to Brussels? You are still determined to carry out this silly scheme of yours?'

'Yes, I am. And we leave in a few days. Why?'

'Are you not going to offer me a drink?'

With tight lips Phoebe poured him some sherry, and then a glass for herself. She needed something stronger than ratafia after the shock she had suffered when she thought her mother might be ill.

Reginald sipped appreciatively. 'Not bad. Not bad at all. I'm going to Ghent to see this fellow Bauwens who's started a new textile industry. We can do business. So I thought, why not spend a few weeks in Brussels. It's near enough to Ghent. And it would be a treat for Hermione and Dorothy to spend some time there, meeting people they could not meet in Yorkshire. As it happens one of my best customers is staying there and has offered to have us stay at his house. So I need his lordship's direction, if you please, miss.'

Phoebe stared at him in astonishment. She was dismayed at the thought of possibly having to meet Reginald and his sisters in Brussels, and could not imagine what he wanted with the earl.

'Jane and Mama will be alone in Yorkshire. You are leaving them alone?' she asked. 'Will they be all right?'

'Of course they will. With a houseful of servants, and friends all around. That isn't alone, so don't be missish. Jane is perfectly capable of dealing with everything in my absence.'

'Yes, of course, I know that. I'm not sure when the earl will be back in London, but if you would like to leave your own direction, I could let you know when he comes.'

'That won't do. I need to see him at his own house, not wait on your convenience.'

Phoebe, hoping it would get rid of him, gave him the earl's address, and without a word of thanks he turned and left the room.

Oh well, she consoled herself. Brussels would be quite large, and as Reginald did not move in the same circles as Beatrice's friends, there was every chance she could avoid meeting him and his sisters.

★　★　★

Lady Drayton's coachman drove them to the party at a house in Albemarle Street, and said her ladyship had told him to come back for them at eleven.

'Oh, but that's far too early,' Sally protested.

'You have been ill, remember, and must not tire yourself,' Phoebe told her, a warning in her voice. 'I know I will be tired and longing for my bed by then.'

Sally heaved a deep sigh but said no more, and Phoebe congratulated herself. She had hated to do it, but knew that if she were to control Sally's wilder activities, she needed a hold over the girl. She had reluctantly threatened to tell Beatrice about the attempted elopement if Sally did any other stupid thing while they were in London, and Sally, laughing at her and calling her an old maid, had promised she would be good.

Sally had chosen to wear one of her new

gowns, in lemon silk, and despite Phoebe's suggestion that a necklace of gold links plus a silver chain on which depended a single pearl, together with pearl eardrops and several bracelets, were not in the best of taste, Sally had laughed and said she wanted to show Emily her jewellery.

Phoebe herself, conscious of her role as companion, had on a demure gown of dark green, and wore, on a simple gold chain, a locket containing miniatures of her parents. Sally had offered to lend her a pair of coral eardrops, but Phoebe, inwardly shuddering, had declined. She saw she would have to work hard if she were to be proud of Sally's appearance in Brussels, but hoped the girl would learn better taste from seeing what fashionable women of the *ton* wore.

There were a couple of dozen people in the drawing-room when they were announced, predominantly young men and girls, but a sprinkling of older people Phoebe assumed were their parents. Emily rushed up to greet them, and dragged Sally away, saying she must meet some of her dearest friends.

Very soon Phoebe realized the party was mainly for playing cards. As several small tables were being set up Emily, coming back to talk to Phoebe, with Sally and a couple of young men in tow, explained there would be whist for those who preferred it, and in another parlour a table for a game of five-card Loo.

Sally opted for Loo, a game which Mrs Kingston had enjoyed occasionally with her cronies in Buxton. Phoebe had always regarded it as insipid, with no need for skill. Dr Kingston had taught her whist, so she decided to join one of the tables in the drawing-room while Sally went off with Emily and her friends to the parlour.

It was two hours before supper was announced, and Phoebe was hungry. She had been concentrating hard, and managing to hold her own with an elderly couple and a middle-aged man who complained that there were no good players in the village where he lived, and he had to come to London to be sure of a good game.

They finished the game and rose to go down to the dining room. As they passed the door to the parlour they heard shrieks of laughter from the Loo players. Emily's mother smiled, commenting that they must be enjoying themselves.

'Then we will have first choice at the buffet,' an elderly man whose rotund stomach seemed to be encased in creaking corsets, commented.

It was more than ten minutes before the

Loo players appeared. They were all laughing, Sally rather loudly, and Phoebe hoped she had not indulged too freely with the wine the footmen had been passing around while the guests were playing.

Sally sat with Emily at the far end of the room, and it was not until a footman came to tell them their coachman was waiting that Phoebe noticed she had removed her jewellery.

'Have you left any of the bracelets behind, or are they all in your reticule?' Phoebe asked, as they waited for their cloaks to be brought.

'It's all right,' Sally said. Her spirits seemed to droop as she said farewell to Emily, promising to write and tell her all about Brussels.

They climbed into the coach and settled in opposite corners. Phoebe's thoughts reverted to Reginald's visit. She hadn't previously wondered why he was so eager to see the earl, but now she did, and hoped it would not lead to more contact with him and his sisters in Brussels.

Phoebe pushed the thoughts out of her mind and asked Sally if she had enjoyed herself. 'It's years since I played whist. I've had little opportunity since my father died.'

'It was all right. I'm tired,' Sally said irritably, and Phoebe wondered if she had been reminded of George, while mixing with several young men. She was thankful when they reached home and she was able to wish Sally a good night and retire to her own room.

★ ★ ★

Zachary returned to his house late the following night. It was some time before he could retire, as there were several messages which needed replies, and a long report which had come from Brussels, and which he needed to read before he went to the ministry to receive his final instructions.

On the following day he had to finalize his plans for Brussels, so in the afternoon he went to visit his sister. As he turned the corner into Brook Street he saw a man he didn't recognize being admitted to the house. When he arrived himself the man was still in the hall, demanding to see Sally Benton's parents.

The butler gave him an anguished look, and Zachary stepped forward.

'Sir, will you come with me? Perhaps I may be able to help you,' he said, taking the man's arm and guiding him into the small parlour.

The man was in his thirties, his clothes were good but rather flashy. He sported several fobs, an enormous emerald ring, a quizzing glass with a pearl-studded handle, and a rather large diamond nestled in his cravat.

'Are you the jade's guardian?' he demanded, shaking himself free of Zachary's hold. 'You're not old enough to be her father.'

'I am not her guardian, but she is staying with my sister. Miss Benton's father is not in London. What did you want with him?'

'Him, her, anyone who's responsible for her. I want the money I won from the cheating jade; a hundred pounds, it was, which she was supposed to pay me yesterday.'

'Pray, sir, sit down. I know nothing of this. Let me introduce myself. I am the Earl of Wrekin, and this is my sister Beatrice Lady Drayton's house. You are?'

The man glared at him. 'My name's Tobias Hill. I let the jade give me notes two evenings ago, when she ran out of money and jewels and couldn't pay her debts. I should have sent her from the table if I'd known she would cheat me.'

'Ah, I begin to understand. Where was it this took place, and what game were you playing?'

Mr Hill told him, and Zachary nodded his head. 'Was the play honest?' he asked quietly.

'Honest! Are you accusing me of card-sharping?'

'By no means, sir, but was it wise to permit a green girl to continue playing, as you seem to have done, and go on winning large sums from her? Sums which you might have expected her to be unable to pay? And do I understand you also won jewels from her? It does not seem the behaviour of a gentleman.'

'I wasn't the only one winning from her, but it was to me she gave her notes of hand. If you're responsible for her, I'll take it kindly if you'll settle her debts. Debts of honour, mind.'

'Pray, wait here. I need to speak to the young lady.'

'You're saying you don't believe me?' He pulled a bundle of slips of paper from his pocket. 'Here, look at these if you think I'm lying, add up the total yourself. One hundred and five pounds it is.'

'I believe you,' Zachary said, 'but I need to see Miss Benton before we have further discussion.'

He left the parlour and walked slowly up to the drawing-room, where he found his sister and Phoebe.

'Where is Sally?' he demanded.

'Welcome, Zachary,' Beatrice said gently, and he gave a rueful grin.

'My apologies. That chit makes me so angry I forget my manners. I see you are better.'

'What has she done now?' Phoebe asked.

'Were you with her at this party the other night, where they played cards?'

'Yes, but why has that put you in such a pother?'

'She is being dunned by some fellow I suspect is a card sharp for a hundred pounds she is supposed to owe him.'

Phoebe went pale. 'There was no gaming there,' she said.

'Were you with her all the time?'

Phoebe shook her head. 'No. I played whist, and she and some of the others played Loo, in another room. But we did not play for money, and I was unaware they did. That explains it, I suppose,' she added to herself.

'Explains what?'

'Pray don't shout at me, my lord! When we came home she was not wearing her jewels. It sounds as though she pledged them, too. But she is just a girl. Can she be forced to pay?'

Zachary was pacing about the room. 'In honour she should, but it's more than she can afford even if she has no pin money for the next year or more. Where was this party? I am going to see the people who allowed such a thing to happen to an unprotected girl. You, madam, should have been taking better care of her!'

'Come now, Zachary, how could Phoebe have guessed what was going to happen at what she had expected to be just a simple evening party with friends?' Lady Drayton asked. 'Emily's parents are respectable people, or I would not have permitted them to attend.'

He swung round. 'I am not blaming you, Beatrice. You were not there, but Miss Kingston was, and she ought to have been taking better care of Sally. If this is the best she can do she is not fit to be in charge of her in Brussels. I mean to ask Cousin Philomena to take her place. She lives in Kensington and can be ready in two days. You can go back to Yorkshire on the stage, Miss Kingston, while I go and tell Emily's parents what I think of them!'

6

Phoebe sat down on a chair near the window.
How could Sally have been so idiotic? She
did not wonder that the earl was furious with
her for not taking better care of her charge,
and knew she deserved to be sent back home.
It was hard, though, after all her dreams of
seeing Brussels, and later perhaps having the
chance of another position so that she need
not live with Jane.

Sally entered the drawing-room cautiously,
glancing from Phoebe to the earl, and biting
her lip.

He was standing in front of the fire,
tapping his fingers on the mantelpiece, his
expression grim.

'You — you sent for me,' Sally whispered,
and crossed the room to where Beatrice sat
on one of the sophas. 'Ma'am, I — I — '

'Gently, child. Come and sit beside me.'

Sally did so, clutching her aunt's hand
nervously.

The earl took a few steps towards her and
Sally drew back against the arm of the sopha.
'I have a fellow downstairs who maintains you
owe him a hundred pounds. Is it true?'

Sally gulped. 'I didn't know it was that much.'

The earl seemed to be controlling his temper with some difficulty. 'Even at Loo it seems an inordinate amount to lose in one evening.'

'I — I had no money with me. They said I could pledge my jewels.'

'Who said?'

'This man.'

'Tobias Hill?'

'Yes, I think that was his name. He — when they said they were going to play for money he lent me some, at first. I didn't have any with me. And . . . and when I lost it, and all my jewels too, and I wanted to stop, he kept saying the luck would turn if only I played on. But it didn't,' she wailed, turning and burying her face in Beatrice's bosom. 'Every time he said I had a winning card and I didn't pass, I lost.'

'He saw your cards?' Phoebe asked, horrified.

Sally glanced at her. 'Well, yes, he said he'd help me. I hadn't played before, you see.'

'I see you're an unutterable little fool!' the earl said. 'He was obviously cheating you. I suppose he won the pool?'

Sally nodded. 'Several times.'

Lady Drayton squeezed Sally's hand.

'Gently, Zachary. The child was in a difficult position.'

'Which she would not have been in if Miss Kingston had been taking proper care of her.'

'I couldn't stop once he made me give him notes promising to pay! I knew I'd never be able to pay him unless I won some money back.'

The earl began to pace up and down. 'You were supposed to pay him yesterday, according to what he says.'

'But how could I? I don't have any money left from this quarter's allowance, and even if I did it wouldn't have been nearly enough. And I don't have any jewels to sell.'

'So you proposed to leave for Brussels and cheat him, did you? Have you not learned that gambling debts are debts of honour? Unless you can prove he cheated you.'

Sally shook her head. 'It was only a game. I thought he'd be satisfied with my jewellery, and forget the rest. I'm sure the jewels were worth more than he said!'

'Quite possibly. Very well, I will settle this, on condition you never again play cards for money.'

Sally sniffed and nodded. 'I don't want to,' she muttered. 'It wasn't exciting, it was horrible.'

'If you have to buy the jewels back for her,

Zachary, Sir William will recompense you,' Lady Drayton said.

'Exactly what did you give him?'

Sally told him. 'And I promise never to do it again.'

'You will have no such opportunity. My cousin Philomena will be accompanying us to Brussels, and she will make a far better guardian than Miss Kingston, who will be going back to Yorkshire tomorrow.'

Phoebe looked up at this. She had not expected to be sent away so abruptly, then she recalled they were to set out for Brussels in two days, so really she had to leave tomorrow. She took a deep breath.

'I will go and pack,' she said, rising to her feet.

Sally was staring at her in dismay. 'Phoebe? Aren't you coming with us? Why not?'

'Because I do not consider her a fit person to have the responsibility of controlling your behaviour.'

At this Sally leapt up and confronted the earl, stuttering in her fury. 'B-but what I d-did has nothing to d-do with Phoebe! She wasn't in the same room! How could she have known? Oh, you're b-being so unfair! Why should she lose her job just because I did s-something stupid?'

'Sally,' Phoebe said, 'it's all right. I

understand his lordship's anger and disappointment in me. I should have been aware of
the possibility when I knew you were going to
play Loo.'

'It was all my fault!' Sally began, when the
door opened to admit the butler.

'My lady, a gentleman to see you. Are you
at home? He says he is a neighbour from
Yorkshire. A Mr Reginald Bradshaw.'

★ ★ ★

Reginald, careless of the conventions of polite
society, had followed the butler upstairs and
now pushed him aside. His clothes, though of
the finest materials, were not a good cut.
Already the coat was straining over his
increasing paunch, and there was what looked
like a soup stain, imperfectly removed, on his
somewhat florid waistcoat, the bright red
stripe clashing with his florid complexion.

'Of course they are at home, my man, and I
don't have the time to waste. My lord, I
called to see you and was informed you were
here. Lady Drayton, I trust you are well. My
wife and her mother sent best wishes if I
should meet you. My lord, I came with a
suggestion. May I sit down?'

Not waiting for an answer he sat down
heavily on one of the smaller chairs, and

Phoebe heard it creak in protest. She herself sat down again. She was curious to see what Reginald wanted with the earl.

'Mr Bradshaw, I assume,' the earl said, returning to stand before the mantelpiece, stretching one arm negligently along it, and Phoebe thought she had never before heard him use such a haughty tone. It had no effect on Reginald's self-consequence, however. He beamed up at the earl.

'Aye. Well, my lord, I heard you were travelling to Brussels soon, and I'm taking my sisters along. We're to stay with Sir James and Lady Potterton. He's one of my best customers and they've taken a house there. I mean to visit this Bauwens fellow in Ghent, on business. So I thought we might travel together. Extra safety, you know. A few extra men, me and my valet, and the coachman.'

'The road from here to Brussels is hardly infested with highwaymen; you will be perfectly safe, Mr Bradshaw.'

'As to that, there are some desperate old soldiers about since they were all dismissed last year. We've had a few cases up in Yorkshire, begging, attacking travellers. And my sisters can help look after your niece. They're older than young Phoebe here, know more of the world, you see.'

'Sally is not my niece,' the earl replied, and

Phoebe almost heard the gratitude in his voice.

'Oh well, whatever. I understand you are taking her to live with her father. In fact, with Hermione and Dorothy travelling along too, you don't need another chaperon, or companion, or whatever Phoebe is called. You could send her back home, where she'd be far better employed helping my wife with the children.'

'Really?'

Reginald was unstoppable. 'If we take two coaches, you and Sally could travel with us, and all the servants, mine and yours, in the second. That would be more comfortable than having to share with a valet and maid, now, wouldn't it? We're putting up at the Clarendon, we could all meet there.'

'By your plan, sir, there would be five of us in one coach. Rather an uncomfortable crush, I'd have thought.'

'No, no, the girls can sit together, they'll not take up a lot of room. Well, what do you say?'

'Mr Bradshaw, you are kind to suggest it, but I have made my arrangements. I always intended to ride, my valet can ride on the box with the coachman, and their maid with Sally and Phoebe.'

Phoebe threw him a quick glance, but he

was not looking at her. Sally spoke.

'Then you will allow — '

'Enough, child. Miss Kingston, may I suggest you and Sally should be supervising your packing? I will talk to you later about the other thing.'

He strolled across to the door and held it open. In a daze, only partly aware she had been reprieved, Phoebe crossed to the door, followed by Sally.

'Come and see me in the library when your brother-in-law has gone,' he said quietly as Phoebe passed him. 'Sally, too.'

★ ★ ★

Sally managed to suppress her giggles until they reached her room. 'Did you see Zachary's face?' she spluttered. 'When your dreadful brother-in-law suggested they travelled in the same coach?'

Phoebe was frowning. 'Am I to come with you after all?' she asked. 'He told us to pack, but I would have to if he is sending me back to Yorkshire.'

'I think he changed his mind when Mr Bradshaw told him to send you back to Yorkshire,' Sally said. 'Mama told me, when we knew he was to escort me to Brussels, that he likes to get his own way, and if he sent you back now Mr Bradshaw would claim the credit. He could never endure the thought that your brother-in-law would think his advice had been taken by an earl!'

'Then I will have to be grateful to Reginald?' Phoebe chuckled. 'Well, I don't mind that, so long as I don't have to travel with them. I hope we don't have to meet them in Brussels.'

'Phoebe, I'm sorry. I never meant to get you into trouble. But it was so difficult, I didn't know how to stop. It would have been so awkward, breaking up the game, and looking silly and childish.'

Phoebe thought the last reason was probably the most important to Sally, but she forbore to comment. 'We ought to be packing. I suppose the earl will send for us when he is ready.'

★ ★ ★

Mr Bradshaw, Zachary decided, was like a persistent wasp determined to attack the rotting fruit. He ignored all hints that his visit had lasted long enough, and did not depart until Zachary, growing bored, told him when he intended to start for the coast. If they had to endure his company on the journey, at least it would be in different carriages, and he himself would be riding. Looking at Reginald's well-fed flesh he did not expect him to sit a horse in any but exceptional circumstances.

When the man finally departed Zachary went thoughtfully back to Mr Hill, waiting impatiently in the parlour.

'Well, sir?'

'Not well, sir. Miss Benton informs me you were aware of the cards she held, and advised her to continue playing even when she did not hold winning cards. Then, it seems, you managed to win the pool whenever it was particularly large. Most of the other players were young and inexperienced, I understand, who might not have understood what you were doing. I don't think you would be welcome in polite society or your clubs if this tale were spread about. In the circumstances I see no need to pay you anything. In fact, I will require you, as a condition of my keeping silent, to return the jewellery you took from Miss Benton.'

'That's slander!' Mr Hill gasped. 'I'm no cheat, and I'll thank you to withdraw that accusation or I'll see you in court.'

'Somehow I doubt it. A man of your years and experience advising a girl who has never before played for high stakes, and advising her to your own benefit, is hardly likely to gain the approval of the courts. Your direction, sir? I will send a man with you to bring back the jewellery.'

He blustered, but in the face of Zachary's calm determination, finally shrugged.

'You don't need to do that,' he said, and pulled a small drawstring bag out of his pocket. 'I have them here. No hard feelings, I hope.'

Zachary opened the bag and tipped out the jewellery. It was all there, so he nodded, crossed to the bell pull and rang for the butler.

'Bring some sherry, please. And ask Lady Drayton's coachman to come to the library.'

When he had poured Mr Hill some sherry, he excused himself and went into the library next door, where the coachman was waiting. He wished he had his tiger for the task, but he had walked to Brook Street, so had to use whoever he could. Beatrice's coachman was burly and looked sensible. He explained swiftly.

'I need to know where the man who is about to leave the house lives. Can you follow him for me? Without being seen?'

Luckily the man was quick witted, and nodded. 'I'll go and hang about on the corner,' he said briefly.

Zachary smiled. 'Good man. I'll keep him

for a few minutes longer.'

Mr Hill, when he returned to the parlour, was pouring himself another glass of sherry. Expansively he held out the decanter and another glass.

'No hard feelings, my lord. Drink with me?'

Zachary accepted the glass, put it to his lips, but did not taste the sherry. He would not drink with a cheat like Hill, but these few minutes would help the coachman get round to the corner of the street. He would ask one of his own footmen to keep an eye on Hill while he was away, if possible by becoming acquainted with one of Hill's servants, and alert him if the man did anything suspicious.

Finally, looking regretfully at the decanter, Mr Hill departed. Zachary poured his sherry into a convenient vase, hoping it would not kill the flowers, and went to the library to confront the two girls.

★ ★ ★

Phoebe sat in a small chair, nervously twisting her hands together, as they waited for the earl to join them. When he entered the room she glanced up at him and was relieved to see a rueful grin on his face.

He tossed the bag with the jewels to Sally.

'I persuaded him to return these. He knows better than to dun you any more.'

Sally fought back tears of relief. 'Oh, thank you! I promise I won't be so stupid again.'

'I'm sure you have learned your lesson. Now, Miss Kingston — '

'Am I to go back to Yorkshire?' Phoebe interrupted. She thought he had overcome his anger, but she needed reassurance as soon as possible.

He chuckled. 'I had every intention of sending you back until your appalling brother-in-law told me to do so,' he admitted. 'I don't appreciate being told what to do by pompous, self-satisfied men like him! Oh, but I beg your pardon. I should not be abusing a relative of yours like this.'

'I told you that was it,' Sally said in triumph.

Phoebe, relieved, laughed. 'As far as I am concerned you may abuse him as much as you like. I don't have a good word to say for him. Thank you, my lord, and I promise I will take better care of Sally.'

'If she permits it! But you have promised to be on your best behaviour, have you not?' he asked, turning to Sally.

She nodded. 'Do we have to travel with the Bradshaws?'

'That depends on them. They know when

we are setting out, but they will be in another carriage, and there will be other people on the road. The entire *ton* seems to be travelling to Brussels. I am sure we can avoid them.'

Phoebe hoped so too, and when a series of small problems delayed their departure by an hour, she expected that Reginald, with his penchant for punctuality, which had so irritated her in Yorkshire, would be ahead of them.

They bade a fond farewell to Beatrice, who would be travelling back to Yorkshire on the following day.

'I can never thank you enough for giving me this chance,' Phoebe told her.

'You deserve it, my dear. And when you come back, if you need another position, I will help you to find one.'

As they drove away Phoebe wondered what she had meant. Of course she would need another position. She had either to earn her living or return to be an unpaid governess at the Bradshaws'. She put aside that thought. It would be months before she need consider it, she hoped.

The two girls, and Annie, were delighted with the scenery, marvelling at the width of the Thames as they crossed over the new Westminster Bridge.

'No houses,' Annie said. 'I thought there

were houses all along the bridge.'

'That was London Bridge,' Phoebe told her.

'Allus thought it were odd having houses on a bridge.'

'Earth has not anything to show more fair,' Phoebe said dreamily.

'Phoebe? What do you mean?'

'Mr Wordsworth's poem,' Phoebe told her. 'He wrote it here, several years ago.'

'You're not a blue stocking, I hope? Phoebe, you can't be!' Sally sounded horrified.

'I like some poetry. But how he can have said it was all bright and glittering in the smokeless air I can't imagine,' she added, looking back at the city and along the river towards the docks, where thick smoke blotted out views of many of the buildings.

'It's all the fires, using that dirty seacoal,' Annie said.

'Perhaps he wrote it in the summer. I can't recall. But I was reading about the bridge in a book in Beatrice's library. It was designed by a Swiss, and opened five and sixty years ago. It's three hundred feet longer than London Bridge and — '

'Phoebe, stop! Who wants to know all that tedious stuff?'

'Well, all those figures and measurements

were boring, but I wanted to know how they managed to build bridges; how they could stop the water for long enough to build the supports.'

'Well, I don't want to know. It's enough for me that we can drive across it. I wonder what the country is like in Kent? And whether the boat will toss much and make us ill?'

'Don't, Miss Sally!' Annie said. 'The very thought of all that water makes me queasy.'

They relapsed into silence which lasted while they drove through Lambeth and took the Canterbury road. When they stopped to change horses Phoebe looked around her at the busy inn yard, then groaned.

'Oh no! Sally, don't show your face. Reginald and his sisters are just coming out of the coffee room and getting into their coach. If he sees us he'll want to travel on together.'

★ ★ ★

Zachary forced himself to smile when Mr Bradshaw hailed him. He'd hoped to avoid the tedious man.

'We thought you'd set out early,' Reginald said, 'and somehow we'd missed you. My two ladies were late getting ready, but are not all the ladies dilatory? I expect your Sally delayed you.'

'No I did not!' Sally said, poking her head out of the carriage window. 'I was ready in good time, and so was Phoebe.'

Reginald laughed, shaking his head. 'If you say so, my dear. I would never contradict a lady. But we can wait while you have some refreshments. Tolerable coffee they have here. Then we can go on together. I'll just have a word with the coachman.'

There was nothing for it. Zachary escorted a simmering Sally and a Phoebe trying hard not to laugh into the coffee room, and ordered coffee and hot rolls. When Dorothy and Hermione, descending from their coach, came in and joined them, fluttering their eyelashes and asking him eager questions about Brussels, he tried to answer politely.

'I have never been to Brussels before,' he said, when asked to describe the town. 'I know no more about the geography and the architecture than you do. No doubt you will soon find your way around.'

'Are you staying with Sally and her father, or at the embassy?' Dorothy asked.

'I'm not sure what arrangements have been made for me. There may not be room at the embassy, but they will have found me lodgings somewhere.'

'So you don't know where. But no doubt we will meet frequently. We hear there are parties every day, and everyone walks and drives in the parks, like they do in London.'

'Do you wish you were still in the army?' Hermione asked. 'I do so love the uniforms, they are so smart and colourful.'

'I can assure you they do not remain so in battle,' he replied.

Zachary happened to glance at Phoebe and saw she was struggling to contain her laughter. What the devil amused her in this situation, he asked himself, and suddenly it dawned on him she was laughing at him and his attempts to evade the sisters' questions. Then Reginald came in and her expression changed, became wary. She really did not like him, and he did not blame her. Having now endured Mr Bradshaw's company for even a short time, he appreciated her desire to get away from his home. The man was an encroaching bore. He was thankful he had not sent her back to the dreadful man's house. She would have found it difficult, no doubt, to escape for a second time, and Mr Bradshaw would soon have returned to Yorkshire. He devoutly hoped so. If he were forced to endure the company of any of the Bradshaws for any length of time, he would find it hard to remain polite.

7

Mr Bradshaw insisted on leading the way in his coach, to the irritation of Phoebe and Sally, for their chaise was faster, but as Mr Bradshaw's coachman held firmly to the centre of the road they were unable to pass him.

'I hope Zachary goes to a different inn when we have to change horses,' Sally said, but he was riding ahead and she could not call out to him.

Her hopes were dashed when it was time to change horses and their coach pulled into the next inn yard. Once more they all descended and went to the coffee room, where Mr Bradshaw was loudly ordering the waiters to set extra chairs about a table.

Phoebe found herself seated between the sisters, while Mr Bradshaw claimed Sally's attention. Annie, the two valets, and Ella, the maid the Bradshaws had brought along, were relegated to the far end of the table. Zachary, refusing the seat offered him by Mr Bradshaw, said he had things to attend to outside, some problem with the coach, and escaped.

'He is so handsome,' Dorothy sighed. 'I believe he is very rich, too. Do you know if he is betrothed?'

'I haven't the slightest notion,' Phoebe replied. She doubted it, or surely his sister would have referred to it, but she had no intention of encouraging Dorothy's manifest interest in the earl. She considered Dorothy. The younger of the two sisters, small and thin, five and twenty years old, and to the best of Phoebe's knowledge, never having had an admirer, she would have as little chance of attracting the earl as would a kitchen maid. She was petulant at home, simpering in company, and appeared to have no interests apart from her clothes.

The earl, Phoebe decided, would eventually have to marry, for all men must want heirs. From what his nieces had said at Ridgeway Park, he disliked his uncle Jonas for some reason and would not wish him to inherit. He would choose as his bride a beautiful, young, rich and well-born girl. He would have had his pick of each year's debutantes, and was clearly difficult to please, for there must be many girls matching those criteria every year.

She sighed. Would she ever marry? Would she find a man willing to overlook her advanced age, her lack of fortune, her birth which was respectable, but no more, and her unremarkable looks?

The sisters were bickering, leaning forward to speak across her.

'Why did the earl leave the army, Sally?' Dorothy asked.

Sally looked puzzled. 'He had to, when his younger brother Francis was killed at Badajoz three years ago. He had been wounded three months earlier at Ciudad Rodrigo, and was recuperating in England.'

'But I don't understand. Why did the death of his brother make him leave the army? Was he afraid of being killed too?' Dorothy asked.

'Of course he wasn't afraid! He's a gentleman!' Sally said. 'But he has no heir apart from his uncle, and could not risk being killed. None of his family would want his uncle Jonas to succeed!'

Phoebe was wondering what was wrong with the coach that kept the earl out in the yard for so long. Was he deliberately avoiding Reginald? She did not blame him, only wishing that she could find an excuse to do the same.

Sally was looking bored, and Phoebe caught the occasional words. Reginald, it seemed, was telling her about his mills, and how he had built them up, expanded and improved them since he had inherited them from his father. She stopped listening to anyone, lost in dreams of Brussels, still not really believing she was on her way there.

The earl came back just as they were finishing. He said everything was now all right, and standing at the end of the table poured himself a cup of coffee, drank it down swiftly, and turned to leave the room.

'We will be ready to go in five minutes,' he told them.

Phoebe went outside and stood looking at the busy scene. It was a large inn, catering for the many travellers on their way to and from the Continent, and must have increased its custom enormously since the fall of Napoleon had opened the way for English people to travel once more. Through an archway she could see another stable yard, which looked very new, though the stables there seemed to be fully occupied.

'Come along, miss,' Annie said, and Phoebe turned to smile at her, then climbed after her into the coach.

Sitting on the seat facing her she saw the Bradshaws' maid, Ella.

'Where is Sally?' she demanded, trying to suppress a feeling of panic.

'Mr Bradshaw suggested she rode in their coach,' Annie said, her disapproval plain.

Phoebe turned to get out again. She could not permit this. But the door had been closed, the steps folded, and the coach began to move.

Did it really matter, she asked herself as she sank back on to the seat. The Bradshaws were not trying to kidnap Sally. The two coaches were travelling in tandem, Sally would be perfectly safe, and there was no need for her to make a fuss.

★ ★ ★

They must have acquired a better team of horses, Phoebe decided, for the coach was bowling along at a much faster pace than before. She put her head out of the window, saw the earl riding some way ahead, but could not see the Bradshaw coach in front. Glancing back, she saw that it was following this time, and dropping further back. How irritating of Sally. Phoebe could have sworn she was thoroughly bored with Reginald and his sisters, so what in the world had possessed her to join them for part of the journey? But for this they might have been able to leave the Bradshaws behind. Now they would have to stop once more at the same inn.

Ella was looking embarrassed, and as Phoebe sat back on her seat began to apologize.

'I'm sorry, miss, but Mr Bradshaw don't

like having to share the coach with the likes of me,' she said. 'He always tries to send the servants in a separate coach, but it weren't possible this time, with just the two of us.'

Phoebe stifled her indignation. It was not Ella's fault that Reginald now regarded her as a servant and fit only to travel with the maids and valets. Doubtless he considered he was helping Sally by putting her with himself and his daughters.

She was silent until they reached the next inn, then, as soon as the coach stopped and the steps were let down she climbed out and ran back to the archway leading on to the road, looking for the Bradshaw coach. It was nowhere in sight.

The earl had followed her. 'What were you thinking of, letting Sally travel with the Bradshaws?' he demanded.

'I didn't. That is, I didn't know she wasn't in our coach until it was too late to stop her. She won't come to any harm.'

'That wretched girl! I heartily wish I had never agreed to escort the two of you to Brussels.'

'Where are they?' Phoebe asked, ignoring him. 'There are so many coaches I can't see if they are coming.'

'I made sure we had better cattle for this stage,' the earl said. 'They will take longer, their team was mismatched.'

'It won't happen again, if I have to tie her to me.'

He laughed. 'Somehow I doubt young Sally could be held if she didn't want to be. Come and have something to drink. Do you want more coffee or would you prefer some wine?'

Phoebe shook her head. 'I'll wait here, but I'm sure Annie and Ella could do with something.' The earl was taking this latest of Sally's exploits more calmly than she had expected, she was thankful to see. Really, the girl could come to no harm, but it was irritating of her to behave so carelessly.

He was about to turn away when a man driving a ramshackle gig pulled up beside them.

'I've a message for some earl,' he shouted, 'but I can't leave this nag. Do you know if he's here?'

'I'm the Earl of Wrekin.'

'Coach broken down a couple of miles back. Snapped pole. They want another sent to fetch 'em. Or a cart. Mighty lot o' baggage they've got.'

'You can't blame Sally for this!' Phoebe began, but the earl held up his hand to silence her.

'Have I said I do? Many thanks for your message,' he shouted after the driver of the gig, who was already thirty yards away. 'Thank goodness it's only a couple of miles. I've a good mind to make the wretched girl walk. Go and tell the others, please, while I organize a rescue.'

Marvelling that he was blaming neither her nor Sally, Phoebe went into the yard where Annie, Ella, and the earl's valet were standing wondering what was happening. Swiftly she explained, then led the way into the coffee room and told them to order what they wanted.

It was an hour before the others arrived. Sally was clearly in a temper, and the earl's expression was grim. Had they quarrelled? Or were they simply annoyed at the delay?

Sally flung herself down in a chair next to Phoebe. 'That man!'

'Mr Bradshaw?' Phoebe asked, thinking it was just as likely Sally was referring to the earl. 'Why did you go with them?'

'I didn't realize it was their coach until I was in it,' Sally said, glaring across the room to where Reginald and his sisters were talking to the innkeeper. 'It's the same colour as ours. It looks the same, and Annie was going on and on about how she was sure she would be sea sick. I was standing where I couldn't hear her. It was too late to get out, and your coach was leaving anyway.'

'Well, you're here now.'

The earl came in, said a brief word to Reginald, then sat down opposite them. Sally looked mutinous, but his expression had lightened.

'The Bradshaws will have to put up here for the night, while a new pole is fitted. Thank goodness we have booked rooms for the night at Dover, so we will not miss the packet with all these delays. Are you ready to go?'

Sally suddenly grinned at Phoebe. 'Oh dear, we'll have to go on without them. What a shame.'

⋆ ⋆ ⋆

The rest of the journey passed without further incident, to Phoebe's relief. She and Sally were entranced with their first experience of a foreign country, while Annie complained bitterly that she couldn't understand a word of what people said to her. The Bradshaws, Phoebe was glad to see, had missed the packet and would have to come on the next one.

Eventually, as it grew dusk, they arrived at Sir William's lodgings, a small house close to the Grande Place. They were shown into a pleasant drawing-room on the first floor, and the footman who had answered the door said he would fetch Sir William. When he arrived, after a pause which made Phoebe wonder if he was in the house, or had to be fetched from elsewhere, he greeted his daughter coldly, looked Phoebe up and down and frowned.

'Your mother writes that you have been making a great nuisance of yourself,' he told Sally. 'She wants me to find some fool who will marry you for your money. I am warning you, if you do not behave as a properly brought up young lady should, I'll wash my hands of you and send you to your aunt Sophronia in Scotland.'

Sally paled. 'I will behave, Papa,' she said, in the meekest tone Phoebe had ever heard her use.

Phoebe wondered what there was about this aunt to make Sally, for the first time since she had met her, afraid. She had little time for wondering, however, as Sir William turned his gaze on her.

'As for you, Miss Kingston, you don't look capable of controlling my daughter, but I will have to put up with you, for now. If I find you are performing your duties inadequately, I will employ some older lady who will know how to do it.'

'Miss Kingston may look young and pretty and fragile, but she is fully capable of making

Sally heed her,' the earl said, his tone amused.

Phoebe shot him a startled look. He had given no indication he thought her pretty, and as for her capabilities, this was not what he had given her to understand he believed. She was nevertheless grateful for his support. Sir William was, she considered, an odious man, and Sally was greatly to be pitied, having him and her uncaring mother as parents.

Telling them he had to go out, he was late for an appointment and would see them in the morning, Sir William departed. The earl also took his leave, promising to call on the following day to see how they did. A maid was summoned to show the girls to two small bedrooms on the third floor, where someone had already put their trunks. Phoebe, slightly hysterical, wondered where on earth Sally was going to put all her clothes, there was so little space.

'There is a meal in half of one hour,' Jeanette, the maid, told them, her accent so strong they had to concentrate hard to understand it. When Phoebe spoke to her in French she smiled in relief, said she would show Annie where she was to sleep, and would then bring up hot water for them to wash.

Phoebe expected Sally to be downcast by

the reception her father had given them, but when they had been served supper in the ground-floor dining room the girl was cheerful.

'Papa has always been stern, but he does not mean half his threats,' she confided. 'He will introduce us to people, and take us to parties, for he does not want to have to keep me for too long. But I will not marry anyone just because he wants to be rid of me.'

'Who is Aunt Sophronia?' Phoebe asked. 'And what can she do to you?'

'She's mad. She lives in the Scottish Highlands, in a very isolated and cold castle,' Sally explained, shivering. 'We only went there once, when I was about ten years old, but it was dreadful. It's dark and gloomy, with almost no furniture and no hangings. Most of the windows have no glass, just shutters. It's on a cliff at the edge of a lake. They call it a loch in Scotland. It's so close I was afraid the castle would fall in. The only fire is the kitchen one, for cooking, and it smokes dreadfully. She goes to bed when it grows dark in winter, and will not permit anyone to have candles, so we had to go to bed too. And she does not eat anything but fish and oat cakes and porridge. She never drinks wine, or even milk, just some horrid fiery spirit that makes you choke. She only

147

has two servants, an old couple who are as crazy as she is, even though she is supposed to be very rich, because she inherited a fortune but never spends a penny if she can help it.'

'Why does she live like that? What does she do to occupy herself?'

'She weaves endless shawls, and in winter wears half a dozen of them to keep warm. She spends the rest of the time fishing in the loch. Papa says she was crossed in love when she was sixteen, and has never recovered, never left the castle since then.'

Phoebe reflected that Sally herself, deprived of George, did not seem unduly concerned. Being crossed in love was clearly not going to make her lose her wits.

'Did she not have parents?'

'I think they died when she was quite young. They were dead when I went there to visit.'

'Then if you don't want to be sent there again you must not annoy your father.'

Sally grinned. 'Don't worry, Phoebe. He won't know where we are half the time, if we are careful. He'll get some dowager to take us to parties, and if we keep out of his way he won't know what we are doing.'

★ ★ ★

Sir William may have found their presence unwelcome, but Phoebe had to admit he did his best for them, during the first week, at least. He took them to visit many of the fashionable people staying in Brussels, and they were soon deluged with invitations to parties, balls, receptions, routs, the theatre, and rides and drives in the Park and the surrounding countryside.

The entire town seemed to be given over to social activities. Besides the English there were many people of other nationalities, though most of the French aristocracy, she was told, had returned to France after Napoleon's abdication the previous year, when King Louis XVIII had been restored to the throne.

She was eager to explore the town, but Sir William knew nothing of its history and dismissed the buildings as old and uninteresting. Phoebe planned to explore on her own, perhaps when Sally was occupied with some of her new friends. They had both been made welcome, and Sally was soon engaged with several girls of her own age, riding, shopping, or just trying on their new gowns and experimenting with different ways of arranging their hair. After a while, when Sally had behaved impeccably, Phoebe felt justified in permitting her more freedom on some of these unexceptional occasions.

They saw nothing of the Bradshaw sisters for more than a week, and then met them at a ball given by Lord and Lady Corby, the parents of Sally's new friends Jane and Deborah. The Corbys, Sally explained with a grimace, lived in Yorkshire and Deborah had told her Mr Bradshaw had called on them and asked Lady Corby to keep an eye on his sisters while he travelled to Ghent to see the man who was building a textile industry there. The sisters were wearing the same gowns they had worn at Ridgeway Park, but they had added more rosebuds so that, Sally said with a giggle, they looked rather like a flower garden.

Phoebe was wearing one of her new gowns, of cream crêpe Lisse, which she had bought in London, and a coral necklace her father had given her on her sixteenth birthday.

Hermione, the moment she saw Phoebe and Sally enter the ballroom, came across to them.

'We were devastated, missing you at Dover,' she said, 'and you did not give us your direction here. We have been trying to discover it ever since we arrived. Will you come to tea with us one day soon?'

They had to accept, but escaped as soon as they could. Rather to her surprise, Phoebe soon found her dance card full. She had, when she accepted the position of companion, imagined she would have to sit with the chaperons while Sally danced, but Beatrice had made her promise she would not refuse invitations to dance.

'Sally needs to think of you as a friend,' she had said, 'someone she can trust and confide in. She won't do that if you sit with the dowagers and remind her you are older.'

Phoebe wondered whether the Earl of Wrekin would be at the ball. They had not seen him since their arrival in Brussels, and Phoebe assumed he was only too thankful to be rid of responsibility for them. He was probably immersed in diplomatic duties. Even if he did attend any of the balls or parties they had been invited to, she did not expect him to do more than give them a polite greeting. So far, however, they had not met, and despite telling herself not to be ridiculous, she could not help feeling just a little disappointed.

When the guests went in to supper, Phoebe saw Sally with a group of young people, including a couple of cavalry officers stationed with the British expeditionary force which had been in Flanders since the end of hostilities. They were all clearly in high spirits, and making rather a lot of noise as they talked and laughed. The wine was flowing freely, and Phoebe hoped Sally was being sensible and not drinking too much. She doubted it, however, and when she saw one of the young men repeatedly refilling Sally's glass, decided she had to intervene. Sally would resent it, but it was her duty. She was pondering the best way of approaching it when the earl suddenly appeared and after a brief word of apology to her partner, joined their group and sat beside her.

'How are you enjoying Brussels?' he asked. 'Sally seems to like it.'

'Too much,' Phoebe replied, frowning. 'She's too excited. I have to detach her from that group, before she disgraces herself.'

'And she will hate you for it. Leave it to me.'

He strolled across to the group, joined in the talk and laughter for a few minutes, and then brought Sally across to her.

'Phoebe, may we go riding in the morning? The earl says he will escort us and show us where the French bombarded the town in — oh, I don't know! Years ago.'

'Twenty-one years since, child. Well, Miss Kingston, have we your permission? Sally tells me her father has provided you both with riding horses.'

'It — that would be delightful,' Phoebe

said, casting him a look of gratitude. The musicians were starting to play again, and people were drifting back from the supper-room.

The earl picked up Phoebe's dance card and glanced at it. 'I was hoping for the pleasure of a dance with you,' he said, 'but I can see I will have to arrive early in future. Is Sally behaving herself, not dancing more than she should with one man?'

'Yes, of course. She has been taught the proper way to behave, and I am confident she has no wish to flout conventions here. Her father has threatened her with Aunt Sophronia.'

He gave a crack of laughter. 'That should keep her in line! Lord Drayton went once with his sister to visit the lady, and Beatrice has not stopped shivering whenever she is reminded of the visit.'

'Is she as bad as Sally says?'

'I don't know what Sally has told you, but she is probably worse!'

Phoebe's next partner, a young man a couple of years older than herself, then appeared to claim her. The earl moved away, and she did not see him again during the evening.

★　★　★

Zachary, back at the embassy where he had reports to read, wondered why he had invited the girls to ride. He had gone to the ball for a short while, obliged to appear because the Corbys were acquainted with his sister. He had seen how Sally's high spirits were leading her into potential indiscretions, and sensed Phoebe's reluctance to spoil her relationship with the girl. It really would have been better if Beatrice had employed a more mature woman to control Sally. It was not fair to give Phoebe the responsibility. She was hardly more than a girl herself.

Despite his reluctance, he found himself enjoying the ride the following morning. It was the end of February, a lovely spring day, Sally comported herself calmly, and Phoebe, clearly delighted, asked sensible questions about the recent wars.

They rode out to the ridge to the west of Brussels, from where the French had bombarded it before occupying the town.

'Why did they come?' Phoebe asked.

'Some supporters of the revolutionaries led a revolt against the Austrian rulers. The town was occupied by the French until last year. In the beginning, they stripped it of whatever they could because their finances were in trouble. Then, a year or so later, they made the Southern Netherlands part of France.'

'I assume they were not popular!'

Zachary heard Sally heave a great sigh. She was clearly bored with the history lesson, but he had no intention of stopping his conversation with Phoebe, who was genuinely interested.

'Indeed not. They took land from the Church and sold it, but what really offended the people was the conscription of their young men into the French Army. Napoleon at least realized how they felt, and restored some of the Church's privileges, but began to pay the priests wages instead of the tithes they had been used to.'

'Oh look,' Sally interrupted, 'there are Jane and Deborah Corby.'

She waved vigorously and the two girls, together with some friends, men as well as girls, rode across to join them. The same two cavalry officers who had been with Sally at the ball were there, and Phoebe wondered whether they ever had military duties to perform. Zachary dropped back, and he and Phoebe, excluded from the chatter and laughter of the younger people, were able to converse as they followed.

'Have you seen much of Sir William?' he asked.

'He took us to meet his friends at first, but once we began to receive invitations, he said he had other things to do. We sometimes see him at parties, but he is with older people, and usually he goes to the card-rooms.'

'Have you met him with a Madame Antoine?'

'I've seen him with several women, and their husbands, but we haven't been introduced.'

Zachary was thoughtful. Should he confide in Phoebe? But she was a sensible girl.

'Lord Drayton is concerned at the state of his sister's marriage,' he said abruptly. 'We have heard Sir William has been paying too much attention to Madame Antoine, who is a young widow, while his sister cares for little but her building plans. He suspects Sir William wants a divorce, and has tried to implicate his wife and the architect. He has not been well lately, and Beatrice fears the scandal in the family, if there is a divorce, will kill him. Will you tell me if you discover any suspicious circumstances?'

'I won't spy on Sir William!' Phoebe said. 'How dare you ask me to do such a thing? He is my employer, but even if he were not I think spying in such a way is despicable!'

'I'm not asking you to act the spy! You misunderstood me. All I ask you to do is tell me if the two of them are spending time together. If there is anything to worry about I will take care of it.'

'You mean you will interfere, and in the process probably lose me my position. No, my lord, you can do your own spying. I will not help you!'

She dug her heel into the mare's flank and cantered after the group of young people. Zachary cursed himself for his carelessness. Beatrice had begged him to try and discover the true state of affairs, and he had thought Phoebe might be in a position to help, but he had misjudged her badly. Well, he would have to rely on his own observations. He went to many of the parties which Sir William might be expected to attend, and he would watch him and the lady they suspected of engaging Sir William's affections.

★　★　★

Phoebe tossed restlessly. She had come to bed hours ago, but could not sleep. Did Sally's father really intend to divorce her mother? She knew little about it, and the topic was discussed, if at all in her presence by her mother's Buxton friends, in hushed, disapproving tones, though Phoebe had detected an air of excitement in the gossip. She had understood divorce was an expensive and difficult process, involving Acts of

157

Parliament, but she did not think it was easy. She had heard of a couple of cases, and no one could have avoided the gossip when, five or six years ago, Lady Charlotte Wellesley had eloped with Lord Paget. They were both well known and the affair had caused much comment. She was sister-in-law to the great soldier, Wellington, created a Duke less than a year since, and he was the eldest son and heir of Lord Uxbridge. Phoebe thought most men asked for divorce when the ladies concerned had run away with their lovers. Lady Benton had not done so. And surely she would not take her architect as a lover, so what possible grounds might Sir William have? Of course, Napoleon had divorced Josephine in order to marry Marie Louise, but that was in France, where he had been ruler and probably able to arrange matters how he wished.

If it happened, would Lady Benton be dependent on Mr Cowper? Would her dowry be returned to her? Would Sir William have to make her an allowance? Phoebe turned the pillow, trying to find a cool spot. She did not know the answers, and told herself it had nothing to do with her anyway. She tried to rid her mind of the questions, only to find herself thinking of the earl. Would he be so offended by her attitude that he would refuse to acknowledge her? His responsibility for

Sally had ended when he delivered her to her father. They would meet only at parties, and he did not appear to attend many of those. He was probably too busy with whatever diplomatic work he was involved in. Would she have an opportunity to dance with him, or would he ignore her if they met? Though gratified her hand had been in such demand her dance card had been full, she would have abandoned every partner if only she could have danced with him.

She sat up and punched the pillow angrily. Her indignation surfaced again. Whatever Sir William intended, she was determined she would not act the spy at the behest of the Earl of Wrekin. How dared he suggest it to her!

★ ★ ★

Zachary was exceptionally busy during the next few days, and when he did have an hour or two to spare did not feel inclined to spend them at any of the parties or balls to which he had been invited. Instead, he took his horse and made solitary rides into the countryside. He avoided the fashionable *parc*, for he did not feel at all sociable. He was also, he admitted, reluctant to meet Phoebe again so soon. He had been a fool to try and involve her, and if he had reflected for longer he would never have spoken to her about his suspicions. It was no wonder she had been disgusted with him. Perhaps, if he avoided meetings for a while, she would have forgotten, or at least forgiven him. He did not explore his motives for wanting her to resume the friendly accommodation they had reached, after his first hostility towards her. It was true he still thought she was too young to be given the responsibility of controlling Sally, but he had to admit that so far she had managed the girl well, probably better than an older woman whom Sally would undoubtedly resent.

He also wished to avoid Lady Mickleton, who had arrived in Brussels a few days before and sent him an urgent invitation to dine with her. She had clearly not accepted that he had no further interest in her. He would refuse all her invitations, but could scarcely help meeting her at balls and other social occasions. At least there, she would not be able to make the kind of scene she was prone to in private.

He rode out early one morning, just after dawn, his thoughts on a letter he had received from Beatrice the previous day. She told him she had heard from Clara in the middle of February. While still absorbed in her building plans, Clara had mentioned that her architect had dismissed his nephew and assistant, though he would not tell her why. She was annoyed because he needed someone to do the simpler jobs, and while he had to do them himself her plans were delayed. Zachary wondered whether the young man would have the temerity to come to Brussels in search of Sally, and knew he would have to seek out Phoebe to warn her.

Sally had not appeared unduly cast down by the foiling of her attempted elopement, and he was certain the pair had been given no opportunity at the time to make plans to meet again. But there were letters, though he shrank from the notion of advising Phoebe to monitor Sally's correspondence. He grinned ruefully. She would regard it as another form of spying and undoubtedly refuse to do it.

Beatrice had gone on to ask how the girls were enjoying Brussels. Mrs Kingston, she reported, was well but was missing Phoebe, and she had invited the lady to stay with her for a few days. This Mrs Kingston felt unable to do at the moment, as she did not feel it right to leave Jane while her husband was away. Had Zachary met Mr Bradshaw in Brussels? She had found his encroaching ways in London aggravating, and trusted her brother had been able to dispense with his company.

Zachary grinned again. As he attended so

few social occasions, and it seemed as though the Bradshaws were only invited to the largest, least select affairs, he had only seen them in passing, nodding acknowledgement, but able to avoid conversation. He hoped Phoebe was not being bothered by them, but he knew that if they had the slightest opportunity they would presume on their relationship. Phoebe was able to move in the best circles, thanks to Sir William, and they would doubtless expect her to be able to introduce them to people they might otherwise never meet.

He must, he told himself firmly, stop worrying about her. She was a competent young woman, perfectly capable of managing her own life. She might even meet some suitable man here in Brussels, one who would ignore her lack of fortune, and her deplorable relatives, and marry her.

His hands tightened on the reins and his horse, taking it as a signal, began to gallop. He gave the animal its head for a while until the beast began to tire, then he pulled it to a walk and turned back towards the town. He had work to do.

He had lodgings a little way from the embassy, and returned there for breakfast, and to change from his riding clothes. Then he walked towards the embassy, forcing himself to forget Phoebe and Sally and their concerns, and concentrate on the work he had to do.

There were more people about than normal in the ground-floor rooms, milling about and chattering. The excitement in the air was palpable. One of his colleagues saw him and walked across.

'Have you heard?'

'Heard what? What's happened?'

'The Emperor, Bonaparte, has escaped from Elba and landed in the south of France a week ago. No one knows for sure where he is, but they say he is marching towards Paris.'

8

Zachary was walking back to his lodgings late that afternoon when he was approached by the Bradshaw sisters. They were clinging to one another, and the word that came into his mind was fluttering. Although they were in their mid-twenties, and looked it, they insisted on dressing like debutantes. This afternoon, though, it seemed they had dressed with less care than usual. Hermione's hat was askew, and her hair was escaping from beneath it in untidy strands. Dorothy, he noticed, was wearing gloves of different colours.

'Oh, my lord! We were coming to find you, hoping you would be at the embassy,' Hermione said, catching her breath and almost choking on the words.

'Is anything the matter?' he demanded, immediately thinking something had happened to Phoebe, and these women were, if not related, connected to her. Though why might they think he would be concerned?

'Napoleon! That monster! He's coming here!' Dorothy stammered.

'Of course he isn't,' he tried to reassure her.

'But they are all saying he's escaped from that island, and is back in France. What shall we do?'

It was a question they had been asking themselves all day long at the embassy. 'We don't know where he is, but he will soon be captured again. The French people have had enough of war. There is no need to do anything.'

'We want to go home.' It was clear they were not listening to his reassurances, and he had heard of a few families who were already packing their bags and leaving Brussels. At the embassy they all thought this an unnecessary and premature reaction, and Zachary was aware that any encouragement to flee might start a general panic. This would, while not a disaster, perhaps convince the French that Napoleon was still to be feared.

'What does your brother say? You should depend on him. Does he wish to return to England?'

Hermione gulped. 'He's in Ghent,' she almost sobbed. 'He went there yesterday, to see this man Bauwens again. He said he'd stay there for a few days because the man is somehow being difficult. Oh, my lord, what shall we do? Should we send for him? Or ought we to pack and go there? It's halfway to

Ostend, we could be on our way home.'

Zachary tried to be patient. 'The news will have reached him by now, I am sure, and if he is concerned he will certainly come back here to you. If you try to go to him you might miss him on the road. It would be best if you waited here until he tells you what to do.'

Dorothy smiled tremulously and clasped his hand. 'Oh, my lord, I knew we were right to come and talk to you. And we really don't want to have to leave, we are having such an interesting time here.'

He extricated himself with some difficulty from her convulsive grasp. 'I suggest you forget all about Napoleon. He'll soon be back on Elba, or in an even more secure place. Now, ladies, I must bid you farewell, I have work to do.'

Hermione was looking far more cheerful. 'If that is what you advise, then we will certainly do so,' she said, simpering. 'Will you be going to the Atkins ball tonight? I think we might go there, Dorothy, as his lordship reassures us there is no danger.'

'I will have to see how my work goes,' he said hurriedly. He had no intention of being inveigled into asking either of them to dance. He had found, on an earlier occasion, when out of duty he had done so, that he had to ask both of them, and as well as being poor dancers who forgot the steps and confused everyone else in the sets, they had no sensible conversation.

Why, he pondered, as he walked away from them, did he expect intelligent conversation during a dance? Most girls he favoured with invitations had little to say apart from gossiping about their friends and others at the ball, or the weather, or what they had been doing to amuse themselves. Phoebe didn't. She made intelligent remarks.

He wondered how she and Sally were reacting to the news of Napoleon's escape. They would not be in a panic as the Bradshaws were, he was convinced, but would Sir William seize the opportunity of sending them back home? He had been forced to accept their presence, but this might provide a perfect excuse to be rid of them. He had no further responsibility for them, but if they were being sent back to England, would Sir William be able to find suitable travelling companions, or a reliable escort for them? He turned his footsteps towards Sir William's house. It would do no harm to go and ask.

★ ★ ★

Phoebe and Sally were eager for reliable news. Rumours of Napoleon's escape, his recapture, his vanishing, had been circulating all day in Brussels, and they had heard all sorts of versions from callers and the servants, who had been out either shopping or simply gossiping with other servants.

Sir William, when he came back to the house in the afternoon, had been abstracted, but when Sally had asked him if he knew any details, he frowned and shook his head.

'It won't affect us,' he told them, and went off to his study, saying he had letters to write.

'So he won't try to send us home,' Sally said.

'Did you think he might?'

'Yes, but he would have to come with us, and he doesn't want to do that while Madame Antoine is here. I dare say if she decided to flee to England he would want to go.'

'She isn't English,' Phoebe said, recalling what the earl had asked her to do. 'Why would she want to flee there?'

Sally grinned at her. 'You ought to listen to the servants,' she said. 'Jeanette told me her father was English, and she was born there. Her mother was Belgian, but fled to England with her parents when the French captured Brussels. She'll have relatives there.'

They ought not to be gossiping, Phoebe thought, but was reminded of the suggestion of the earl's that she spy for him. Did he know this? Angrily she told herself it was neither her nor his business, and tried to distract herself with a book. It was no use. Sally kept wandering to the window, watching people in the street, though what she could discover from that Phoebe did not know.

Sally did, however, see the earl's approach.

'Now we'll know what's really happening,' she said with satisfaction, and went to sit down by the fire and pick up the copy of *La Belle Assemblée* she had been looking at. 'The Earl of Wrekin is coming in.'

Phoebe suddenly felt hot. They had not seen him for several days, and she had been feeling neglected, though she told herself she had no cause for it. When they attended balls she was never short of partners, though she was always hoping he would be there and would ask her to dance.

Jeanette, without coming to ask if they were at home to visitors, showed him straight into the drawing-room. Sally began to ask questions before he had taken a seat.

'Jeanette, please bring tea, and some of that cake Cook made this morning,' Phoebe said. 'Sally, have patience. His lordship will tell us why he is here in a minute.'

Sally looked at her, a disgusted expression

on her face. 'Phoebe, you want to hear the news as much as I do.'

The earl laughed. 'And so does every person in Brussels. I can only tell you what I have heard, that Napoleon is landed in the south of France. But you need not be concerned. He will soon be recaptured.'

'Then we don't have to go home?'

'Why should you? It's a long way from the Mediterranean to here. Does your father wish you to go?'

'No, he says there is no danger, nothing to fear. But Henry — that is, Sir Henry ffoulkes, he's one of the cavalry officers stationed here with the army — says most of the army was dispersed after Toulouse, after Napoleon abdicated a year ago. There is just a small army here.'

'That's true. Some of our best troops were sent to America, or the Indies, and many of the men were discharged. But Bonaparte has no army at all.'

'The Duke was here in August, wasn't he?' Phoebe asked.

'He surveyed the defences on his way to Paris to take up his ambassadorship there, yes. There is a line of defence between us and France. It was just a precaution, as some Frenchmen think they should still be in control of Flanders, and it is likely the people who are negotiating at the Congress in Vienna will not agree.'

'So we can forget Napoleon.'

'Indeed we can, and you may attend the ball this evening with no qualms. Miss Kingston, will you save me the supper dance?'

★ ★ ★

That evening, at the ball, there was little else talked about but Napoleon's escape. Phoebe was startled to discover there was considerable sympathy for him amongst the French who were living in Brussels.

'He was good for France,' one lady told her. 'What did the Bourbons ever do for the people?'

'But the wars he started, the thousands of men who were killed, that would not have happened if he had not wanted to conquer other countries.'

'He only fought the people who threatened him. He did many good things. The ordinary people are — how do you say it? — better off than they used to be. He stopped the excesses of the revolution. There is now good law in France.'

'I don't understand it,' she told the earl later when they had danced and were eating supper. 'Some of them sound as though they want him to become emperor again.'

'It is mainly those people who are living here. The monarchists went back to Paris when Louis was restored to the throne. But there is no need to worry, he won't come here.'

'I'm not concerned about that. Sally is friendly with some of the soldiers in the army stationed here, and surely, even if he could gather together some of his old supporters, our men would stop them. And the Belgians do not want to come under French rule again.'

'How is Sally behaving?' he asked, and Phoebe thought he was trying to change the subject. Of course, working at the embassy as he did, he would be privy to information others did not have, but he might not be free to divulge it. What she had been hearing was mainly uninformed speculation.

'She is not repining for Cowper,' she told him. 'The attentions of the young men here, particularly the ones in scarlet coats, seem to have distracted her most successfully.'

He laughed. 'And what about you? Are there any young men paying you attention, distracting you?'

Phoebe was startled. 'I am not on the catch for a husband, my lord. I'm a mere companion, and attend social functions only because Lady Drayton insisted I kept a close watch on Sally.'

'But surely you would like to be married, with your own home, and not have to return to the Bradshaws' house once Sally is settled?'

Phoebe shuddered. 'I will not do that. I intend to find another position. Sir William, or Lady Drayton, will give me a character.'

Phoebe's next partner came to claim her, and she did not see the earl again. The Bradshaw sisters were present, but apart from stopping for a brief word, Phoebe was too much in demand to spend any time with them, even had she wished to. She had too much to think about, and had almost forgotten the day's rumours. The earl's remarks had discomposed her. Of course she would like to have a home of her own, surely all girls would, but she saw little prospect of it. Just because she was a good dancer, light on her feet, and unlikely to make a fool of herself by not knowing the movements, so that she was a popular partner, did not mean any of the young men who asked her to dance would even consider asking her to be their wife. She had no dowry, came from a modest, if decent background, unlike many of the men and girls here in Brussels, most of whom were wealthy and from aristocratic families.

It was different for Sally, but so far as Phoebe could judge she did not appear to favour any one man. Phoebe was certain she had forgotten Cowper, but Sally seemed to distribute her favours evenly amongst the young men she knew. Phoebe had half expected her to be falling in and out of love every week, but this had not happened, for which Phoebe was truly grateful. The girl needed more time to meet several men before she made a choice, and Brussels was an ideal place in which she could do that.

It was time for the last dance, which Phoebe had promised to an elderly man, a retired colonel who said he had known her father when he took the waters at Buxton. He looked tired, and she suggested they sat out. As they were sitting watching the dancers, a lady Phoebe did not know approached them.

'Colonel, how nice to see you looking so well. And your companion is Miss Kingston, I believe?'

'Lady Mickleton. Yes, you are correctly informed.'

The colonel rose to his feet and bowed over her hand. He did not appear to be overjoyed at this meeting.

'I have a message for you, Miss Kingston.'

'Then I will take my leave,' the colonel

said, and moved away.

Lady Mickleton took his seat and smiled at Phoebe. 'I am so glad to be able to speak to you. Zachary has told me how cleverly you are managing Sally Benton. But I have heard a few other people who are not so approving. Forgive me, child, but I felt someone ought to let you know, and Zachary does not feel it is his place to speak. We are old friends, you understand.'

'What is being said?' Phoebe asked, puzzled.

'Well, you are a paid companion, I think. Some of the highest sticklers are of the opinion you should not be treated as an equal to Sally.'

Phoebe paled. 'They think I should sit in the chaperons' corner, and not dance? Is that what you are trying to tell me?'

Lady Mickleton laughed, and seemed a little embarrassed. 'Well, yes, child. You are very young, and not, I think, accustomed to Society. It's hardly surprising if all the attention here in Brussels has gone to your head. My dear, don't look so shattered. You will not be ostracized, if you take a little more care. I'm not advising you to give up dancing totally, just to be a little more careful not to dance every single dance. Some of the old tabbies will say you are on the catch for a rich husband.'

Phoebe stood up. The music had come to an end.

'Thank you for the warning, my lady. I will, of course, heed it.'

★ ★ ★

On the following morning the Bradshaw sisters were shown into the drawing-room where Phoebe and Sally were discussing the rival merits of primrose or sea-green silk for a new ball gown Sally wanted. Phoebe, still upset over her encounter with Lady Mickleton the previous evening, and wondering if the woman had been right, tried to appear welcoming, but before she could say more than a few words Hermione burst into eager speech.

'Phoebe, have you heard the news? That monster is marching towards Paris. We really have to get out of Brussels. Reginald's friends say they are going within days, and shutting the house, so we will have to go too.'

'Where is Reginald? What does he say?' Phoebe asked.

'He's still in Ghent, and he sent a message to say he was in the middle of delicate negotiations and could not leave, but we must stay here, and if the Pottertons leave, we must come and beg Sir William to take us in until he can come back and find us somewhere else to live. He knows there would be no room for him as well here.'

'There's no room for you!' Sally said. 'There isn't a spare bedroom in this house.'

'Well, we thought you and Phoebe would be willing to share, and we could share too,' Dorothy said. 'Just for a few days. Then no doubt Reginald will be going home, and you must come with us, Phoebe. Jane and your mother would never forgive us if we left you here, in danger.'

Sally, Phoebe could see, was flushed with indignation, and just about to reject this suggestion. She put her hand on Sally's arm.

'Dorothy, don't you think all this is a little premature? We don't know where Napoleon is, and even if he is marching towards Paris, that does not mean he will come on here. The Pottertons may not leave, and if they do Reginald may be back before they go.'

'It's so frightening,' Hermione said. 'Please, Phoebe, Sally, help us.'

'If there is any need we will do what we can,' Phoebe said, and gripped Sally's arm tightly, shaking it a little.

Sally sat back in her chair and glowered, but Phoebe finally got rid of the sisters without promising anything, by suggesting that if they were anxious about leaving

Brussels they should be packing what they could in preparation.

'Of all the impertinence!' Sally almost exploded when they left. 'Asking us to share a room! I've never met them before we came here, and they are only distantly connected with you. They've been encroaching ever since we met.'

'It won't be necessary,' Phoebe tried to reassure her. 'They can be unpleasant if they feel inclined, so I did not want to give them any cause while we are all still here. But I suspect Reginald will head straight back to England if there seems to be the slightest danger. You won't have to refuse them.'

'It would give me the greatest pleasure to tell them exactly what I think of them,' Sally said, her expression mutinous.

'Let your father do it,' Phoebe advised. 'This is his house, he would have to be consulted. Besides, he may decide to leave himself if there appears to be any danger.'

* * *

Zachary was walking through the Grande Place early the following morning when he saw Phoebe, accompanied by Annie, coming towards him. Both carried baskets and had clearly been marketing.

'Good morning,' he greeted them.

'Is there any news?' Phoebe asked. 'We cannot discover anything for certain, but there are rumours that the French are welcoming Napoleon. Is it true?'

'Some are,' he told her cautiously. He did not wish to cause her any alarm, but the news they were hearing from France was unexpected and disturbing. Instead of halting Bonaparte, as he marched northwards at the head of a small band, one regiment had already joined him at Grenoble. 'Where is Sally?'

'She complains of a migraine and is lying in her room with the blinds drawn.'

'Is it the news which has upset her?'

'I don't think so. Her father insists we are safe, and says he has no intention of joining those who have moved to Antwerp, or even gone back to England. Sally is not afraid.'

'I am pleased to hear it. You are not either?'

Phoebe shook her head. 'Of course not. Napoleon has no army, apart from a few attendants, so what can he do?'

Zachary suddenly made up his mind. He enjoyed Phoebe's company, but apart from the few occasions when they had danced together, he normally saw her only when Sally was with her, and Sally's chatter irritated him. Here was an opportunity to get to know Phoebe better.

'Then will you come riding with me this afternoon? I have a few hours free and thought I would go and look at the defences to the south of the city.'

Phoebe looked surprised. Was this the sort of invitation Lady Mickleton would advise her to refuse? Then she tossed her head. She was doing no harm, and if the old tabbies Lady Mickleton said were criticizing her did so, she would ignore them. 'Well, thank you. That would be interesting. I'd love to come, if Sally doesn't need me.'

'If she has a real migraine she will want nothing more than a darkened room and quiet for the rest of the day. I will call for you at two.'

Phoebe was ready for him when he arrived, and they were soon trotting along the Charleroi road, through the Forest of Soigny.

Zachary explained what had been done, but confessed that the British expeditionary force was totally inadequate for dealing with Bonaparte if, by some great misfortune, the former emperor gathered an army about him.

'Wellington came and surveyed the defences last year, but he left the Prince of Orange in charge, and he is not very experienced.'

'He fought in the Peninsula though. He's a general.'

'Yes, because he is a good soldier, and we need the Dutch support, but he is only three and twenty.'

Phoebe laughed. 'My age, my lord, which you thought was too young to control just one young girl.'

Zachary glanced across at her. She was laughing at him, and he grinned ruefully. 'I was wrong. I apologize.'

'But I don't think I would care to be in charge of an army. Why was he put in charge here? He is not very popular, I understand, but I'm not sure why.'

'He was put in charge because we are using Dutch troops. As for his unpopularity, that is mainly because he ignores the Belgians. He prefers to mix with the English and the native Belgians feel neglected.'

'And many of them prefer the French. Some did well under French rule. Is there any possibility there might be some internal revolt in support of Napoleon?'

Zachary shook his head. 'They are officials, in the main, not soldiers. But it is very unlikely Bonaparte will get here.'

They rode for several miles, and Phoebe asked many intelligent questions about Bonaparte and the recent wars. Zachary was surprised when they reached the small village of Waterloo.

'We ought to turn back soon,' he said, 'are you going out this evening?'

'We have tickets for a concert, but if Sally is unwell we won't be going.'

'Then let us ride a little further and have some wine at an inn.'

The wine at La Belle Alliance was thin and sharp, and they did not linger. Zachary escorted Phoebe back to Sir William's house and then went to his own lodgings. He had two rooms on the first floor, plus an attic for his valet. As he mounted the stairs he was surprised to hear voices coming from his parlour. He threw open the door and saw, reclining on a sopha which had been drawn closer to the fire, a slender woman in her thirties, dressed in a white round gown, with a travelling cloak thrown negligently on to a chair. Leaning over the back of the sopha was a tall, grey-haired man, stooped a little from age, his face lined and his cheeks ruddy.

'My dear Uncle Jonas,' Zachary drawled. 'To what do I owe this pleasure?'

★　★　★

Sally declared she was much better after her sleep, and did not wish to miss the concert that evening. When they arrived one of the first people they saw was Sir Henry ffoulkes, who came straight up to them, made his bow, and said he hoped the ladies were not concerned by the rumours of Bonaparte's advance across France.

'We'll stop him,' he said confidently.

'I'm not at all afraid,' Sally declared. 'We have an army here to protect us, and that monster has just a few hundred men supporting him.'

Phoebe was observing the young couple closely, trying not to make it too obvious. Sir Henry, tall and willowy, handsome in a boyish manner, had fashionably cut blond hair. She judged him to be in his early twenties, and he was clearly attracted to Sally. By the way the girl beamed up at him Sally returned his regard. He always seemed to be present at all the functions they attended, and was one of the first to solicit Sally's hand for a dance at balls.

Phoebe decided it was the duty of a chaperon to discover what his prospects were before Sally became too enamoured of him. She felt a twinge of apprehension. Was this spying? She told herself it was nothing like the spying the earl had asked of her, in regard to Sally's father. Ought she to alert Sir William, and ask him to make the necessary enquiries? He was Sally's father, and would have to be involved in settlements and so on.

Then she hesitated. He wanted Sally married and no longer his responsibility. He might encourage Sally without taking due regard of her best interests. Phoebe sighed, and wished Beatrice was there to advise her. Should she write to her friend? She shook her head. There were other young men Sally was friendly with. This might be as short a lived infatuation as the one for George Cowper. Until Sally expressed a definite preference Phoebe could do no more than try to discover whether any of the young men were suitable as husbands.

She must ask the earl. He could make enquiries far more easily than she could. He would not wish Sally to fall into another scrape with an ineligible young man. She pushed aside the uncomfortable reflection that she had refused, and indignantly, his own request for information on Sir William and the lady he was reputed to be dallying with. Perhaps, she thought, she might just mention that she had seen Sir William driving in the Park with Madame Antoine the previous day. The Earl could make of that what he would.

She forgot during the concert, losing herself in the music. Some of the most important artistes were in Brussels, and Phoebe relished the opportunities of hearing them perform. When they reached home again, though, she attempted to talk to Sally, asking her if she knew where Sir Henry's home was in England.

'Oh, Phoebe, I really don't know. Somewhere near the south coast, I think, but we don't talk about that sort of thing. Why should we? He was at several of the battles in the Peninsula, and he tells me all about those. I hadn't known before just how awful the conditions were for the poor soldiers. Phoebe, you don't think there will be more fighting, if Napoleon gathers another army?'

'Everyone seems to think he will soon be stopped and recaptured, so I don't think we need worry,' Phoebe replied.

Sally's lack of interest in Sir Henry's home seemed encouraging. Surely, if she were seriously considering him as a suitor, she would want to know such details? Phoebe decided she need not be concerned. For the time being, she could relax and not have to make enquiries about him.

★ ★ ★

'What brings you here?' Zachary demanded of his uncle.

Zachary glanced at the woman he refused to call his aunt, even by marriage. At the age of sixty Jonas, until then the epitome of a rakish bachelor, had astounded his friends and relatives by marrying the thirty-year-old woman everyone had suspected had been his mistress for the past few years. Clorinda Jacoby, before that time, had made a precarious living on the stage. She was striking but not particularly beautiful, and her talents as either actress or dancer had, so friends had told him, been minimal. The mystery had been solved, to the satisfaction of most of the *ton*, when Clorinda had produced a son barely seven months after the wedding. Some of Zachary's friends had aired their suspicions that Jonas was not the father of the boy, and for three years, ever since Jonas's marriage, his sisters had pressed him with increasing urgency to marry and produce his own heir.

'For you don't want to risk a bastard succeeding to the earldom,' Beatrice had said, and his other sisters had been equally blunt.

'How long have you been in Paris?' Zachary asked now.

'Last April, we went there in time to see fat old Louis come in to take the throne our gallant soldiers had won for him. Clorinda had never been there, of course. She was a child when it was last possible to travel in France.'

Clorinda looked up at Zachary from under

impossibly long eyelashes. 'It was so wonderful,' she breathed.

At that moment a thin wailing cry was heard. Zachary strode across the room and stared down in astonishment at a small baby lying in a straw basket. 'What the devil?'

'No, a little angel,' Clorinda said, smiling triumphantly at the earl, 'another son, my lord.' Then she leant down and lifted the child, pressing him to her breast, and cooing gently to him.

'I assume you are on your way home?' Zachary said, recovering.

Jonas grinned at him. 'You surely don't expect me to remain in Paris and put my dear wife and the mother of my children, my heirs, at risk, do you?'

'Your elder son,' he had to force himself to say the words calmly, 'is in England, I believe.'

'Little Jonas is safe enough, well looked after by Clorinda's own mama. We're taking Zach — we named him after you, as he's in line for your title, after me and little Jonas — for her to look after,' Jonas said, and Zachary shuddered.

He had, on one memorable occasion, met the lady's parent soon after Jonas had married. His younger sister had been in London and given a party. Jonas, not invited, had heard of it and brought his wife and mother-in-law to, he proudly announced, meet their new family. Mrs Jacoby was, she coyly informed Zachary, the principal of a school for young ladies. Zachary had subsequently discovered that the 'school' was a cover for a discreet brothel, patronized by country squires and merchants, in London to sample, without their wives' knowledge, the delights of the capital.

Zachary determined, once more, that he must marry as soon as possible. Now Jonas had two sons he began to look more kindly on the idea. It was inconceivable to think a future Earl of Wrekin might not only be brought up in such a place, but had a grandmother who was a madam. The trouble was, he refused to marry as a matter of convenience. His own parents had married for love, and had created a wonderfully happy home for their children. He wanted to do the same, but so far had met no girl with whom he could contemplate spending the rest of his life.

A vision of Phoebe Kingston came into his mind, and he ceased listening to Jonas, who was explaining again how he intended to return to Brussels once he had taken the baby to London, and wait until it was safe to go back to Paris. Phoebe? She was by turns irritating and companionable. She was intelligent and sensible. He corrected his thoughts. He had only felt irritation because of her youth, or when Sally had done something reprehensible. And on those occasions Phoebe had proved both sensible and competent. She was pretty, but not the raving beauty his friends expected him to marry. And her brother-in-law was a deplorable, toadying bully.

He shook his head. He had no intention of marrying Phoebe Kingston, and he could not think where such a preposterous notion had come from.

9

Three days later Sally once more claimed she had a migraine and wanted only to stay in bed with the blinds down. Phoebe, concerned, wanted to send for a Doctor.

'It isn't natural for a young girl to suffer such frequent headaches,' she said, as she drew the curtains in Sally's room.

'Miss Sally has suffered for the past year,' Annie said, from where she was straightening the bedcovers and tucking Sally in.

'Then it's time a doctor saw her.'

'Mother called one, and he said I'd grow out of them,' Sally whispered. 'Now please, leave me alone! All I need is the peace to sleep.'

'I'll just make up the fire, then you can be left in peace for an hour or two until I need to make it up again, and bring you some broth,' Annie said, provoking a groan from Sally.

'I'm warm enough, and I don't want to be disturbed. I just want to sleep. And I don't want any broth.'

'You need to keep your strength up.'

'Annie, if you don't go away and leave me alone I'll scream!'

'That won't improve your headache,' Phoebe said, but she drew the protesting maid towards the door.

'I'll lock the door,' she thought she heard Sally mutter as she closed it and led Annie along the landing to her own room.

'Annie, how long has she had these headaches?'

'About a year, miss, just after her birthday last April, they started. Sometimes there'd be two or three weeks between attacks, sometimes she'd have a couple or more a week.'

'But her mother's doctor said it was nothing to be concerned about?'

Annie sniffed. 'What did he know? Man-milliner, he were, just came and looked at the poor girl, didn't even touch her head to see if she were feverish. Looked as though he dain't want to get his lily-white hands dirty, if you want my opinion, for what it's worth. Just asked if she ached anywhere else, and that were it. Back to drawing-room and Lady Benton's sherry.'

'Should we call a doctor here?'

Annie sighed. 'We don't know any, and I wouldn't trust one of these foreigners. And she never seems the worse afterwards. Bright as a button, usually, by the evening, ready for a party if there's one going.'

Phoebe decided to leave it for now, but she

would ask about discreetly for a doctor who could be recommended, and if the headaches persisted, Sally would see him, whatever she said.

Annie's mention of Sally's birthday had made her wonder if Sir William would be prepared to give her a party, even a ball. Sally had missed the normal presentation of debutantes in London, where she could have expected a ball for her come-out during the Season, and invitations to those given for fellow-debutantes. It wasn't that she was lacking invitations, they seemed to have more than one for every evening, and there were many daytime functions too, which would increase in number as the weather grew warmer. Already Phoebe had heard of picnics and cricket matches being planned.

A ball for herself, though, was important for any girl, as Phoebe knew. It marked her final passage from childhood into the adult world. Phoebe was not in the ranks of the *ton*, but even her parents had held a special party on her eighteenth birthday. She blinked away a wetness in her eyes as she recalled it. It was only months afterwards that her father had been killed and her life changed for ever.

Sally would no doubt want a part in the planning, but first she had to secure Sir William's permission, and then find a suitable venue, as this small hired house was not at all adequate for a large party. They already knew so many people here, and Sally would want to invite them all. But until these matters were decided she would not mention the idea to Sally. If Sir William refused, she did not want Sally to be disappointed and resentful. She went to find Jeanette and ask if she knew when her master would be at home.

★ ★ ★

As Phoebe had expected, Sally was better by the evening. She had, Phoebe had discovered, indeed locked her door to prevent Annie disturbing her. Meeting Annie on the landing, holding a tray with a bowl of broth and a tisane, she had comforted the maid who complained she was not being allowed to do her duty towards her young mistress.

'Leave her alone; she'll be recovered the sooner if we don't disturb her sleep.'

'She used to do this back at Benton Manor,' Annie grumbled. 'Even as a child, some nights, she'd lock her door and say she wanted to be on her own and not be disturbed by anyone. If I'd been her mother I'd not have allowed it!' she added, stumping away down the stairs.

Sally appeared at dinnertime, and Phoebe

wondered if she might after all be ill, as her cheeks were flushed and her eyes bright.

'I'm quite better,' Sally protested. 'I always am after I've had a good sleep, but Annie just won't accept that's all I need. We're going to the ball tonight. Papa said yesterday he'd be there. I wonder if he's going with Madame Antoine?'

'Don't you mind, the attention he pays to her?' Phoebe asked.

Sally stared at her. 'Why should I? Mama has her friends, why shouldn't Papa amuse himself if he wishes? She's from a good family. It's not as though she's some dubious bit of muslin.'

'Sally!'

'What's the matter? Oh, are you shocked I know about such things?' Sally laughed. 'As far as I can tell almost everyone does it. I daresay I might too, once I've been married for simply ages and want something exciting to do.'

Phoebe could not disguise her shock at this attitude. 'But, when you marry, won't you want to love your husband?'

'Well, of course, or I wouldn't marry him. But I don't think that sort of love can last for ever, do you?'

'I would hope both love and respect would last. Sally, how would you feel if your parents were to be divorced? That would create such a scandal.'

'Oh, they would probably all have to live abroad for a while, but it wouldn't affect me, if I were married by then. And after a while no one bothers. They are accepted by all except the stuffy high sticklers. Look at the Earl of Uxbridge. He is in the House of Lords even though he did run away with Lord Wellington's sister-in-law. They got divorced and married, and they had a dozen children between them to be offended by it.'

Phoebe laughed. She couldn't help it. At least Sally might not suffer unduly if what the earl feared happened.

An hour later they were entering the ballroom. Sally wore one of the gowns she had bought in Brussels, of pale pink crêpe trimmed with white lace on the bodice and white embroidery around the hem. Phoebe, who had been tempted to spend some of the money Lady Benton had given her for clothing, had a plain amber satin gown, embroidered in the same colour on the bodice.

Sally was approached immediately by Sir Henry ffoulkes, who seemed to have been loitering in the doorway to the ballroom, as if to intercept her. He was growing quite particular in his attentions, and Phoebe determined again she must discover more about him. They moved away, watching the dancers. It was a cotillion, and would not finish for some time, so there was time to talk.

Phoebe's opportunity came a few minutes later when the earl came to talk to her. She plunged straight in.

'Sir Henry ffoulkes, with Sally. Do you know anything about him?'

'In the cavalry. Did quite well in the Peninsula, I believe. Is that what you wish to know?'

Phoebe took a deep breath. 'His family, prospects, the sort of things a good chaperon ought to know before encouraging her charge to accept his increasingly persistent attention.'

'Oh, that sort of information? He is not married, not paying special attention to any other girl, and so far as I know not promised to anyone,' he drawled, and Phoebe flushed, recalling his request that she watched Sir William.

'He — his family?' she asked.

'He inherited the title several years ago. It's an old creation, dates at least from Charles the Second. He is comparatively wealthy, owns a good estate in Hampshire, and a hunting box near Melton Mowbray. He has

196

two sisters and a young brother, and his mother is still alive and devoted to him.'

Phoebe blinked. 'You know a great deal, my lord.'

The earl grinned at her. 'I, too, have been watching Sally,' he said. 'Much as the chit irritates me I have her interests at heart. Beatrice would be annoyed with me if I did not answer her weekly letters with details about Sally's conduct. And about how you are enjoying your visit here,' he added.

Phoebe was both pleased and embarrassed that Beatrice enquired about her from the earl. 'I have letters from her too,' she said. 'The latest came this morning, and she is concerned. News of Napoleon's escape had just reached Yorkshire. Jane had driven to Ridgeway Park to ask her advice. Jane had never been there before, but she is very worried for the safety of her husband and his sisters. And me, of course,' she added with a laugh.

'Have you seen Mr Bradshaw? Do you know what he means to do?'

'He called yesterday while we were out, and left a message that he had to go again to Ghent and would call again in a few days. It did not appear he was unduly worried, though his sisters seem terrified whenever I see them.'

'Ah, Zachary, my boy, finding time to enjoy feminine company despite the advance of the monster?'

Phoebe looked at the man who had interrupted them. He was in his sixties, grey-haired and rather stooped, though the padding in the shoulders of his coat disguised this a little. He wore old-fashioned black satin knee breeches, and after a quick glance she decided he certainly had some padding around his calves. His spindly legs could never, by nature, have developed such shapely muscles. His face was badly shaved, whiskers visible in the deep creases that ran from his nose, and on his lined cheeks. His eyes, pale blue and sunken, were scrutinizing her with deep interest.

Clinging to his arm was a slender woman a few inches taller. Much bejewelled, she was in her thirties, simpering and blinking her eyes in a way which would have better suited a shy fifteen-year-old. Phoebe could see traces of cosmetics on her highly coloured face. No lips or cheeks could possibly be that bright without the aid of paint. Nor could her hair, which was almost the colour of brass, be natural. The neck of her bright blue gown was indecently low, and Phoebe, embarrassed, averted her gaze.

'My dear Uncle Jonas. Phoebe, this is my

uncle, the Right Honourable Jonas Walton and his wife Clorinda. Jonas, this is Miss Kingston, a friend of Beatrice's.'

He nodded to her, but looked offended, and Phoebe wondered why the earl had been so brusque and unconventional in his introduction of his uncle and Clorinda. It was obvious he disapproved of her, and Phoebe, after one glance, could appreciate the feeling, but he was not the sort of man who would normally show this so openly and, what's more, be discourteous to a member of his family.

Jonas, if he was annoyed, had soon recovered his temper.

'I'm so glad to have seen you here tonight, my boy. Wanted to tell you I'm taking Clorinda and little Zach to England tomorrow. After all, must keep the heirs of the Wrekin title safe from old Boney, mustn't we?'

He sketched a bow to Phoebe, his gaze never leaving her face, then, with what looked like a triumphant grin towards the earl, swung round on his heels and guided his wife away.

'Damned jackanapes!' the earl swore under his breath, and then took a deep breath. 'My apologies, Phoebe. The thought of that woman's sons possibly inheriting my title makes my blood boil. Her mother kept a bawdy house, and I wouldn't be surprised to know she had once worked in it before she trapped that fool Jonas!'

Phoebe couldn't help laughing at his outraged expression.

'Oh, lord, I shouldn't be talking to you like this!' he exclaimed, clapping a hand to his brow. 'He makes me forget civility. He's welcome to name his firstborn after himself, but I find it insupportable that he names the second after me. He need not look to me to act as godfather!'

'Well, you have it in your own hands to prevent his sons from inheriting,' Phoebe said, 'so if they do you can only blame yourself. You could marry and produce sons of your own.'

⋆ ⋆ ⋆

Zachary continued to reassure everyone who asked that they were quite safe to remain in Brussels, but not everyone believed him. Lady Mickleton was one who did not.

'You want to be rid of me, whatever you say,' she said, when they met at a ball.

'If I did I would hardly be reassuring you it is safe to stay.'

'That is just your trickery. But I know you

don't want me, you have barely spoken to me since I arrived. You are too absorbed with that insipid little chit.'

'With Sally Benton?' he asked, astonished.

'Oh, don't try to pull the wool over my eyes. Not her, it's her little companion I mean. I wish you luck getting her into your bed. She looks a cold fish to me.'

'I have no desire to get Miss Kingston into my bed!' he told her. He had rarely been so angry. 'But I always knew you had a common mind.'

She looked as though she wished to hit him. 'I am going home tomorrow. I do not intend to be caught here when Napoleon arrives.'

The population was changing with more rapidity than he and others at the embassy could keep track of. Many of the English had departed from Brussels, some, like his uncle, for the safer shores of England, others for towns further to the north, like Antwerp, or closer to the coast, like Ghent or Bruges, from where they could, if necessary, flee to Ostend and a ship home. There were newcomers from Paris, people who had been enjoying the social life there instead of in Brussels. Many of these were French Royalists, too afraid of the former emperor to stay with King Louis.

With them they brought news and rumours, but they had no clear notion of Bonaparte's whereabouts, except he was somewhere between the Mediterranean coast and Paris. 'I am not remaining to discover it,' more than one person said to Zachary.

Fortunately they had more reliable news at the embassy, and it was worrying. After some of the King's troops had changed sides at Lyon, many people were beginning to wonder about the rest of the support Bonaparte might still garner. The man clearly had some sort of aura that compelled people to support and obey him. Zachary could appreciate how, in the past, weary from the bloodshed and excesses of the revolution, the French would have welcomed a strong man who could restore order, and even, through his military conquests, give them back some pride in themselves. Did that also apply today? There were many unemployed, disaffected soldiers who might imagine his coming would give back to them employment and self-respect. And after being so thoroughly defeated by the Allies, did they smart and long for a chance of revenge?

Taking a break from his duties, he decided to invite Sally and Phoebe to ride with him, and soon they were trotting sedately in the *parc*, nodding to their acquaintances and stopping to chat with several.

'I long for a fast gallop, not this tedious saunter,' Sally muttered to Phoebe, and then groaned. 'Oh, no, look who's coming! We won't be able to escape them, they're heading straight for us.'

'You can at least be polite,' Zachary told her, though his own spirits had drooped when he saw the Bradshaw sisters, seated demurely in a barouche, being driven along towards them.

Their coachman, poked in the back by Dorothy's umbrella, halted so that his passengers could talk to the riders. Zachary inclined his head, raising his hat, while Phoebe greeted them and Sally, with an air of surprise, said she thought they had gone home to England.

'Oh, no,' Hermione said, and giggled. 'Dorothy has an admirer, so of course we don't wish to leave now.'

Zachary made appropriate remarks, and looked on appreciatively as Phoebe, without a blink, asked for more details. Sally, reprehensibly, had turned aside to hide her expression, and was staring fixedly across the *parc*.

When they were able to get away Phoebe sighed. 'I was hoping, now Reginald is back from Ghent, they would go home. I couldn't see any reason for them to stay.'

'I understood the Pottertons, their hosts, left some days ago?'

'They have, and Reginald was able to move them to a hotel before all the people from Paris came.'

'At least they haven't been urging us to take them in,' Sally said.

'When did they do that? And why should they expect to be able to foist themselves on you?'

'It was while Reginald was away,' Phoebe began to explain, but Sally cut in indignantly.

'They expected us to share, so that they could have one of our rooms. I told them we hadn't enough space, and there would certainly not have been a room for their odious brother. He had the impertinence to tell me, the other evening, that I wore too many jewels for a chit my age. I could have hit him!'

Zachary had at times deplored Sally's lack of taste when, on important occasions, she had loaded herself with, it seemed, all the jewels she possessed, but he had refrained from comment, and could understand her chagrin. He was aware that Phoebe had exercised a great deal of tact regarding Sally's wardrobe, for Beatrice had told him so in her letters, but he could hardly expect Phoebe to be successful in moderating every single aspect of Sally's attire.

When he had escorted them home he went back to his lodgings. He had been aware of the admiring glances Phoebe had attracted from riders and strollers in the *parc*, and discovered his own attitude towards her was changing.

She was sensible, competent, pretty and, so far as he could judge, even-tempered. She was not, however, he told himself severely, someone he wished to make his wife.

★ ★ ★

A few days later, Annie, without pausing to knock, rushed into the drawing-room where Phoebe was writing letters while Sally played idly on the pianoforte. The maid still had on her hat and clutched a shawl round her shoulders. The basket with the meat and vegetables she had been out to buy swung from her arm, and with a gasp she set it down on the floor.

'Annie, what is it?' Phoebe demanded. It was unheard of for Annie, normally so calm and sensible, to behave in this fashion.

'Miss Sally, Miss Phoebe,' Annie gasped, and clutched her hands to her bosom.

'Annie, you've had a shock. Come and sit

down and tell us what's happened. Have you been attacked?'

Sally left the pianoforte and came to push her maid into a chair. 'Sit down, put your feet up on this stool, and take a deep breath,' she ordered. 'The French Army isn't at the gates, is it?'

Annie had recovered a little, and she clutched Sally's hand convulsively. 'Miss Sally, we must pack at once. We have to get out of here!'

'Calm down, Annie. What have you heard?'

'Oh, Miss Phoebe, it's all over the town! More soldiers have joined that wicked man, and he's marching to Paris. They'll murder us in our beds if we don't get back to England!'

'Paris is a long way from here,' Phoebe said calmly. 'I don't think we need be concerned for the moment. Let's wait until we have advice from Sir William or Lord Walton, and if they advise we move they will make suitable arrangements.'

'But it may be too late!' Annie wailed.

'Nonsense. What would you have us do, Annie? Set off to walk to Ostend, without money or passports?'

'We'd hire a carriage, Miss Phoebe,' Annie said, offended. 'I'm not daft enough to tell you to walk!'

'Good. So we will wait for Sir William to

tell us what to do and make suitable arrangements. Now, don't you think Cook will be wanting that meat?'

Annie, with a toss of her head, rose to her feet and picked up the basket. 'I do hope you don't regret this, Miss Phoebe,' she said, as she marched out of the room.

Sally looked after her. 'I don't want to be sent home,' she said in a small voice. 'Phoebe, do you think it's true?'

'We'll soon hear. I think it's likely. After all, where else would he go? If he wants to take power again, and surely that's the whole point of his coming back to France, he has to win control of Paris. If he can drive out the king, people will probably support him.'

'He won't get much further,' Sally said. 'We have the army here, and Henry says that even with Slender Billy in charge the French cannot get past the defences.'

'Slender Billy?'

'You must have heard what they call the Prince of Orange. It was his nickname in the Peninsular, Henry says. I wonder why the Princess Charlotte broke off their engagement?'

She soon went back to her pianoforte, and Phoebe began to worry about the birthday party she was contemplating for Sally's birthday, in the middle of April. She must speak to Sir William soon to see whether he would sanction a ball for his daughter, and trust Sir Henry was right and the army currently in Flanders would be strong enough to hold back any French forces Napoleon was able to send against them.

★ ★ ★

Zachary felt he had enough to do, monitoring the information filtering in from agents in France, without having to deal with his sister's increasingly urgent and plainly spoken letters. This one was even more peremptory than the earlier ones.

She had been informed, she told him bitterly, that Jonas now had two sons, though whether he had actually fathered them she preferred to doubt. In his entire deplorable career she had never before heard a whisper of any progeny, and she had hoped he was unable to produce any. She had heard, she added waspishly, that the sort of unmentionable indispositions men of his sort frequently suffered could render them incapable of reproducing. And she was reliably informed that he had on several occasions had to take some sort of disgusting cure.

He winced at her language. She had made no attempt to wrap up her suspicions. He admitted they could be true. If Jonas had, during his debauched career, never sired offspring, the chances of him producing two sons within such a short time were remarkably slim. Clorinda, from his few meetings with her, did not look to be the faithful sort, and he could not imagine she would be content with the attentions of an old man like Jonas. He, at the moment, was thoroughly infatuated, and she was taking full advantage of this to promote the fortunes of her sons.

Beatrice was blunt.

It is high time you ceased being so odiously fastidious, did your duty to your family, and married. You should have done so after Francis died. Surely there are enough eligible girls who would take you on, and give you sons so that the earldom does not fall into the hands of that harpy! If an accident befell you, and Jonas were to die soon, would you want that wretch in control of your estates and money?

He put the letter aside. In his heart he knew Beatrice was right. He had a duty to his family. He had enjoyed a dozen years of freedom from family responsibility, with pleasant enough liaisons with women who understood there was nothing serious in them, whenever he wished. He was a good, conscientious landlord, but he doubted it would be enough for him to spend his life caring for his estates. Appointing reliable stewards and overseeing their work was all he wished to do, though he would be distressed if he ever lost any of his inheritance. Working for the diplomatic service was satisfying. He took his seat in Parliament and spoke there occasionally, when something he thought important was being debated. An insidious thought crept into his mind. Marriage would not prevent him from following his career. Of course, he would have to abandon his discreet amours, but with the right wife he doubted they would interest him. The problem, as it always had been, was to find the right wife.

Pushing aside any decision, he went to the embassy. There he found all in uproar. Seizing the shoulder of a messenger hurrying past, he demanded to know what all the fuss was about.

'Sir, we've just heard!'

'That seems obvious. Heard what?'

The man gulped, waved the sheet of paper he was carrying. 'Sir, I must deliver this note at once.'

'It will help you on your way if you answer

my question. What is causing all this commotion?'

'It's Bonaparte, sir. Marshal Ney promised the king he'd bring him back to Paris in an iron cage.'

'Yes?' Zachary was unable to go on. Had Bonaparte been captured? Was it all over?

'He's joined him.'

'You mean — Ney has joined Napoleon?'

'Yes, sir, we just heard.'

Zachary closed his eyes. This was desperate news. Bonaparte's appeal to one of his oldest and best marshals had transformed the situation. Before, he would have been relatively easy to overcome. Now, in all probability, Ney's defection would encourage hundreds, thousands more to rejoin their former commander. He would be planning to regain his former conquests in Belgium and Italy. It seemed as though war was inevitable.

10

Phoebe managed to find Sir William alone after breakfast. Sally was in her room trying to decide which gown she would wear that evening, while her father retreated to the small room he called his study. She knocked on the door and was bade enter.

He looked up from some papers he was reading, and raised his eyebrows.

'Well, Miss Kingston? Trouble? Is my daughter causing problems?'

'Not at all, Sir William,' Phoebe replied, trying to keep the irritation out of her voice. Why should Sir William assume, because she wished to speak with him, that Sally was causing trouble? Did he want some excuse for sending them back to England?

'Then what is it?'

'It's Sally's eighteenth birthday in April,' Phoebe told him, and he nodded. 'I wondered whether she could have a party, a dance perhaps, if we can find a suitable venue.'

He looked irritated. 'She goes to balls almost every night, I believe. Why does she need another one?'

'This is her come-out, Sir William. In the normal way she would have had a ball in London, as all debutantes do, to formally introduce them to Society.'

Phoebe felt as though she were instructing some rustic farmer in the ways of the *ton*, and suppressed her frown. Sir William knew what was expected of him. She hurried on.

'This isn't a normal year. Many of the people she would expect to invite to such a ball are here, in Brussels, so I thought it would be appropriate to hold a dance for her here.'

'That's her mother's responsibility.'

Phoebe lost all patience. 'Her mother is not in Brussels, nor likely to be. Do you wish Sally to be deprived of the normal pleasures she might feel entitled to because you and her mother are at odds? I will organize the affair; you need not be concerned in the arrangements.'

'Apart from paying for it, I suppose, or do you intend to provide the means yourself?'

'It seems to me a father's duty to introduce his daughter to the *ton* in a suitable manner.'

He stared at her in silence for a moment, and Phoebe wondered whether she had gone too far, and allowed her annoyance to ruin the prospects of him agreeing. Then he nodded, and she breathed a sigh of relief.

'You are right, I suppose, Miss Kingston, but this house is far too small for the sort of party you envisage.'

'Thank you. I know the house would not do, but I can look for a more suitable room, in a hotel, perhaps.'

'There's no need. My friend, Madame Antoine, has a house with a large ballroom attached. She will be only too delighted to loan it to you. Here,' he added, turning to the desk and writing on a sheet of paper, 'this is her direction, and a note to ask her permission to use the ballroom. Will you arrange it with her?'

Phoebe wanted to protest, and through her mind tumbled distressing thoughts of what the earl would say, but from the sardonic look on Sir William's face she knew that this was Sally's only chance of a ball. If she rejected it, Sally would lose all opportunity of a proper come-out. If she accepted, the speculations about Sir William's involvement with Madame Antoine would be proven correct.

He was old enough to make his own decisions, she decided. His behaviour had already given rise to comment, and he must be aware that this would only fuel the rumours.

'Thank you. I will visit Madame Antoine as

soon as possible and arrange a suitable day with her.'

'Ask for her help. She knows everyone here, what tradesmen to use, and she will be delighted to do something for Sally.'

★ ★ ★

Zachary was kept busy during the following days. News filtered through, and was far from encouraging. As they had feared, Ney's defection from the king's service encouraged others to join Napoleon. More monarchists fled from Paris, and it soon became difficult to find rooms in Brussels, despite many English visitors having left for towns further away from the anticipated invasion.

'He said he'd fight for Belgium, that's what he told a visitor while he was still on Elba, and Brussels is too close to Paris for comfort,' one old lady told Zachary.

On the surface the embassy staff and the military remained calm and tried to reassure people that Napoleon and his army would be halted long before they could reach Brussels. They knew that a wholesale evacuation of visitors would only give comfort to Napoleon's supporters in Belgium, and perhaps increase support for him.

King Louis remained in Paris until the last

possible moment. He finally left in the evening of 19 March, the day before Napoleon once more took possession. Reports came of how Bonaparte had been carried shoulder-high into the Tuileries, without any opposition. And then very little information came through from France.

From Vienna came news that the Congress had declared him an outlaw, then that the powers had formed an alliance against him. To Zachary's relief, the Duke of Wellington was given command of the army in Flanders, and they eagerly awaited his arrival in Brussels. He came at the beginning of April and began the task of financing and positioning the troops he had, while attempting to gather more.

Two men who were not pleased were the Prince of Orange, who had been the Commander in Chief of these soldiers, and his father, King William. They were surrounded by officials who had been in the service of France for many years, but they eventually gave way and reluctantly accepted Wellington's appointment as Commander in Chief.

Zachary was privy to the problems the duke was experiencing, but in public was as reassuring as possible. It was safe to remain in Brussels, he insisted, and truly believed it. If anyone could prevent Napoleon from recapturing Belgium it was Wellington.

The balls and concerts continued, and Brussels was still full of people determined not to show any fear of Bonaparte. Wellington himself appeared on many occasions, and gave his own entertainments.

'He is not at all as I expected,' Phoebe commented on one occasion when she had watched the duke talking to some ladies who all hung on his words. 'I believe he is a ladies' man.'

Zachary laughed. 'Don't all ladies love a hero?'

'His wife went to England, from Paris,' Phoebe said. 'I would have thought it her duty to be with him.'

'I think she can have some influence in London. There are men in the Opposition who dislike him, and they cannot be allowed to hamper him in what needs to be done here. He has problems enough.'

'What sort of problems?'

Zachary found it easy to talk to Phoebe. She was intelligent, asked sensible questions, and swiftly appreciated his explanations.

'The army here is inexperienced, especially the Dutch. Many of our best regiments are unavailable, they are in America or elsewhere. King William will not agree to anything suggested, he seems to delight in being obstructive. Slender Billy resents being superseded by the duke as commander. Wellington was very anxious, before he arrived, in case the prince acted too soon. We are not officially at war.'

'Not? But the armies are gathering, how can we not be?'

'Until one side invades the territory of the other war has not officially been declared.'

Phoebe shook her head in disbelief. 'I suppose that is the legal position, but it seems ridiculous when everyone is preparing to fight.'

'You are not afraid? You don't wish to go home?'

'Everyone who leaves Brussels gives comfort to that monster! Sir William is happy we stay, and I would hate to be thought a coward. Besides, it is Sally's ball next week.'

'I had not forgotten it. At Madame Antoine's,' he said, trying to keep his voice neutral.

'It was Sir William's suggestion, and I could not object without risking Sally not having a dance at all.'

'Of course not.'

Phoebe looked at him rather doubtfully. 'You will come?'

'I will be there. May I have the supper dance with you?'

★　★　★

Phoebe had been surprised at how friendly and helpful Madame Antoine was. She applauded Phoebe's plan, sat down with her to decide what needed to be done, and suggested that since she knew the tradesmen in Brussels who would supply the food and drink and decorations, she would look after all of that while Phoebe and Sally made lists of who was to be invited and sent out invitations.

'And you need to have your gowns made, of course. I will introduce you to my own favourite modiste, and make sure she will complete them in good time.'

Sally chose a pale cream satin trimmed with deeper cream ruching and embroidery around the hem. 'I don't want white,' she decided. 'It makes me look too pale.'

Phoebe chose a sarsenet woven in two shades of pale green, with no trimming other than a darker green ribbon threaded at the neckline and below the bodice. When Madame Antoine came to inspect them she nodded her approval.

'Excellent taste, my dears. Your papa will be proud of you, Sally.'

'I wish Mama were here to see me,' Sally said later to Phoebe. 'She doesn't believe I'm grown up now.'

'Have you written to tell her about the ball?'

'Yes, but she has not replied. I don't suppose she is interested,' Sally said, a wistful note in her voice.

It was the first time she had shown any sign of being concerned by her mother's attitude. Lady Drayton had told Phoebe Sally's mother found her a nuisance, and Phoebe had gained the impression Sally was pleased to be away from home.

'The letter might have gone astray,' she said. 'The postal service between here and England might be having difficulties. So many people are trying to cross the Channel.'

'Do you think so?'

Sally looked slightly more cheerful, but an hour later Phoebe discovered her in the parlour writing a second letter to her mother.

'If the first one went astray, I had better send another,' she said. 'It won't be in time for Mama to reply before the ball, though.'

'You can write and tell her all about it afterwards.'

Sally nodded, but did not seem overjoyed at the prospect. Phoebe went to the bureau and got out her list of all the people who had been invited.

'Have we had any more acceptances?' she asked.

'A few. I put the notes over there. The Bradshaw sisters have accepted, and I was so hoping they might have gone back to England.'

'We had to invite them. It would have been a dreadful snub not to. Has Reginald returned from Ghent, do you know? He went there again after he'd found rooms for them in the hotel.'

'Yes, and he's coming too. Phoebe, he wrote he would be delighted to partner me in one of the country dances. What shall I do? I don't at all wish to dance with him!'

'Then you had better make sure your dance card is full before he asks you. I don't think there will be any problem with that, judging by how many of the soldiers have accepted invitations!'

Sally smiled, then shrugged. 'If they can come. Henry says there are a hundred thousand men strung out to the south of Brussels, but the duke may change where they are positioned. He wants more men to the west, in case Napoleon tries to swing past him. He's putting his more experienced soldiers in between the Dutch and Belgian troops, because many of them are quite inexperienced, and some are mercenaries and perhaps not to be trusted.'

Phoebe smiled to herself to see how Sally, formerly quite ignorant of and uninterested in politics, was now so well informed. It must be the influence of Sir Henry and her other soldier friends.

★ ★ ★

Zachary paused as he saw Reginald Bradshaw on the steps of the house where he had his rooms. Was the man asking for him? He was tempted to turn round and escape, for he found the man tedious in the extreme. Then he decided he might as well speak to him, or the fellow would be pursuing him all over Brussels.

'Ah, my dear Wrekin,' Reginald exclaimed, as he turned away from the door and found Zachary just behind him. 'I was coming to consult with you.'

'Yes?' Zachary knew he sounded unwelcoming. 'I would ask you in for a drink,' he added, 'but I have to go out again immediately.'

'No matter, no matter, some other time perhaps. I wanted to ask you, as someone who may have better intelligence than us mere civilians, if you felt it was safe for my sisters to remain in Brussels. They are so anxious to attend young Sally Benton's ball. I tell them that if you permit her to remain they will be perfectly safe, but the silly pair are in a twitter of apprehension.'

'I don't think they are in any danger,' Zachary said. How he wished he could frighten them away, but it would not serve if at the same time he maintained it was safe for Sally and Phoebe to stay.

'Well, we will remain for the time being. I had thought to remove to Ghent, now that King Louis has set up his court there. I have made so many contacts during my business discussions, there would be no shortage of entertainments.'

'It is closer to the coast if you decide to go to England after all,' Zachary said hopefully.

'Indeed. But I also have dear Phoebe to consider.'

'Phoebe? She is safe enough with Sir William.'

'At the moment, but I would not be doing my duty to my sister-in-law if I permitted her to remain here while danger threatened.'

'You mean you would want to take her back to England with you?' Zachary asked, and suppressed a smile as he thought of Phoebe's probable reaction to such a suggestion.

'Of course.'

'Would she agree?' Zachary asked innocently.

'She would obey me. After all, she has no father, no closer relative to care for her.

Thank you for your reassurance. Now I must permit you to go about your business. There must be so much for you to do at a time like this.'

Zachary stared after him, wishing he might be present at such a confrontation. Phoebe would refuse. But what if Sir William decided Sally should go back to England too? Suddenly the prospect of not seeing Phoebe regularly, not being able to partner her at balls, or ride out with her, disturbed him. Of course, if there really was any danger, he would want her safely away from Brussels, but there was no real threat, yet. He turned and slowly climbed the stairs and went into his rooms, where he poured himself a glass of Madeira and sat in a chair near the window, staring unseeingly at the scene outside.

★ ★ ★

After Sally's moment of home sickness, Phoebe was not entirely surprised that she had another migraine the following day. She refused to eat anything at breakfast, sipped at a cup of tea, and then said she was going back to bed and did not want to be disturbed.

'Please, Phoebe, all I need is to sleep, and I will probably be better this evening.'

Phoebe had plenty to do, making last

minute arrangements for the ball with Madame Antoine, so she walked round to that lady's house and helped her direct the servants who were decorating the ballroom. Large pots with tall trees had been hired, and these were being set out to separate the chairs at the side of the room, creating small alcoves for half-a-dozen people.

'We don't want to make them too small, or the chaperons will be accusing us of condoning illicit meetings,' Madame said, laughing.

'They can hardly be secret when anyone in the main part of the room can see who is there,' Phoebe replied.

During the past few weeks, while she had been working with Madame Antoine to arrange the ball, she had come to like the woman enormously. Her husband, Phoebe learned, had been killed several years ago in a hunting accident. He had, she mentioned one day, been at Oxford university at the same time as Sir William, before the French Revolution, and they had been good friends there.

So that might account for Sir William's friendship with the lady. It might, after all, be just that, and not the liaison people suspected. Phoebe wondered whether Zachary knew this, and whether it made any difference to his fears that Sir William was contemplating a divorce.

It was late afternoon when she returned home, and the moment she entered the house Annie appeared.

'Miss Phoebe, I can't make Miss Sally answer me.'

'She said she didn't want to be disturbed, Annie.'

Annie nodded. 'I know, but she's been abed for hours now, her headache must be better. And she would want to have this straight away.'

Annie was waving a letter around.

'What is it?'

'A letter from her mama, and she's been complaining at not having one, so I thought she would like to get it as soon as possible. But she won't answer me, and the door's locked. Miss Phoebe, I'm worried she's too ill to talk.'

Phoebe thought Annie was making a fuss about nothing. If Sally did not want to be disturbed, it was quite likely she would refuse to answer. But she could see the maid was worried, so she followed her up to Sally's room and tapped on the door.

'Sally, please answer. There is a letter here from your mama.'

There was no reply. Annie bent down and

226

peered through the keyhole. 'The key's been taken out,' she said.

'Well, Sally could have put it somewhere else.'

'Why should she? Oh, Jeanette,' she said as the maid appeared, carrying a pile of linen upstairs, 'is there another key to this room?'

Jeanette laughed. 'All the keys of the bedrooms are the same, they fit one another.'

Phoebe went straight to the door of her own room and abstracted the key. She slid it into the keyhole and it turned easily.

'Quietly,' she cautioned Annie, 'just in case she is deep asleep.'

She opened the door and looked in. The curtains were drawn, but a shaft of sunlight came through a gap and fell across the bed. It was unoccupied, and undisturbed. Unless Sally had remade it, which was highly unlikely, she had not been in it today.

The gown she had been wearing at breakfast was cast over the back of a chair, and her slippers were beside it. Phoebe looked round the room.

'Annie, stop wringing your hands, and let's see if we can discover what is missing.'

Annie, nodding, went swiftly through Sally's clothes. She turned a puzzled look towards Phoebe.

'Her riding boots have gone, but her habit's

still here. And her cloak's gone. None of her gowns is missing. I don't understand.'

'I think I do! Did she bring breeches with her?'

Annie looked scandalized. 'Breeches?' she asked. 'Of course not! Why should she do such a thing?'

'At home,' Phoebe explained, 'Sally used to ride out in men's clothes, because she preferred to ride astride. Did you pack all her clothes when we came?'

'Dressed like a boy! Well, I never!'

'Did you always pack for her?'

Annie took a deep breath 'Pack for her? Not everything, Miss Phoebe. There were so many new gowns, and she wore some of them in London, before we came here, so there was constant packing and unpacking. I couldn't remember what was packed and what was not.'

'Then I think we will discover she has gone riding, secretly, because she knew she would not be allowed to if her father and I knew.'

'Her papa will be furious! He'll send her home!'

Phoebe nodded. 'I'm afraid he might.'

'Then the lass'll miss her ball. How could she be so silly!'

The thought crossed Phoebe's mind that if Sally were sent home in disgrace she would also be packed off to England, and having to look for another position. She struggled with her conscience, trying to decide whether it was for her own benefit that she was inclined to overlook Sally's stupidity.

'If no one knows, there will be no scandal. It would be a pity for her to be sent home now, but we have to stop this. I'll threaten to tell her father if she does it again. And we'll take her breeches away from her!'

★　★　★

Phoebe fetched a book from her own room and sat down to wait in Sally's. She sent Annie away with strict instructions not to say anything to the other servants about Sally's absence. She used the key of her room to lock herself in, and waited.

It was only a short time afterwards that she heard stealthy footsteps approaching, Sally had, she assumed, crept up the back stairs while the servants were occupied in the kitchens preparing dinner.

She laid down her book, and sat facing the door. The key was turned quietly, and the door opened slowly. Sally, swathed in a long cloak that hid her breeches, slipped in, still watching the landing outside. She closed the door softly, inserted her key, and locked it.

Then she turned round.

'Welcome home, Sally,' Phoebe said.

Sally gasped. 'What — how did you get in here?' she demanded, trying, unsuccessfully, to conceal her breeches with the cloak.

'More importantly, where have you been? And dressed in breeches?' Phoebe asked.

Sally took a few steps towards her. 'Phoebe, you know I detest having to ride side saddle.'

'Yes, I know that. Where have you been, and with whom?'

Sally gave a deep sigh, and threw her cloak across the bed. She sank to her knees beside Phoebe and tried to clasp her hand. Phoebe gently removed it.

'Where, and with whom?' she repeated.

'Only with Henry,' Sally said at last. 'No one else knows.'

'So you go out riding with just one young man, in breeches, and think because no one else knows it doesn't matter? Have you so soon forgotten George Cowper? I think you promised then, when you were saved from the consequences of your folly, to behave properly in future.'

'You've been riding alone with Zachary Walton!'

'Not in breeches. Besides, I am older, not a green girl.'

'I'm not a green girl, Phoebe, I know what

I want! This time it's different! I really do love Henry!'

'That does not excuse such behaviour. Sally, don't you see, if it were known you would be ruined. You would have no chance of a good match.'

'But I have Henry. I don't want anyone else, and he wants me.'

'An honest man would have approached your father.'

Sally flared up at that. 'Henry is honest! I asked him not to speak yet, or he would have seen Papa weeks ago. Phoebe, don't you understand, we no sooner set eyes on one another than we knew. He is the only one for me, and it's the same for him.'

'Perhaps. But unless you promise me not to repeat this, I will have to tell your father, and you know what he would do.'

'Phoebe, you wouldn't! He'll send me home! And I have to stay here, with Henry.'

'Do you promise?'

Sally clasped her hands. 'Yes, anything, so long as you don't tell Papa! Phoebe, if you were in love you'd understand!'

Wondering whether she was relying too much on Sally's word, Phoebe said she would not speak unless Sally did something else so imprudent.

'But I will take your breeches,' she said.

'Get them off; it's time you were dressing for dinner. We have invitations to a ball this evening, too.'

Sally reluctantly stripped off the breeches and handed them to Phoebe. 'I truly love Henry, and he might be killed if there is fighting,' she said.

'We must hope not. By the way, here is a letter for you.'

Sally took it, and smiled. 'It's from Mama, at last,' she said, and broke the wafer. She skimmed through the letter and gave a little skip of excitement. 'Phoebe! Mama is coming to Brussels, she'll be here in time for my ball! Oh, that's wonderful!'

★ ★ ★

Zachary tossed yet another letter aside. This time it was from his eldest sister, informing him that Jonas had installed himself, his wife, his mother-in-law and his two sons in Zachary's main residence in Shropshire.

The servants could hardly deny him, Caroline wrote. *After all, he lived there while your father was alive, as he had no country home, though your father would never have permitted him to take such a wife there. When are you going to stop*

prevaricating and find yourself a wife?
Heaven knows, there are plenty of chits
on the catch for you, all you need to do
is choose the most amenable and get her
in the family way as soon as possible.

His sisters did not hesitate to be blunt, he thought, with a rueful grin. The news that Jonas was making free with his property angered him, but there was little he could do about it from Brussels.

He came to a sudden decision. His sisters were right, and he would have to find himself a wife as soon as possible. A picture of Phoebe Kingston came to mind, and for the first time he seriously considered the possibility of marriage with her. She had no dowry, but he was wealthy enough for that not to matter. She was sensible; he enjoyed her company; Beatrice approved of her. They need not see a great deal of her deplorable brother-in-law. Yorkshire, thank goodness, was far enough from all his houses to prevent too frequent visiting.

He would think about it seriously, he promised himself. It was time, however, to get dressed, as he was to accompany the duke to a ball this evening. While working tirelessly to improve his army, and gather more troops, Wellington gave an impression of calm which did a great deal to steady the nerves of both troops and civilians. Part of this was his frequent appearances at social occasions, and the amount of entertaining he did himself.

The ball was at one of the large houses on the outskirts of the city, and the extensive gardens surrounding it were illuminated with hundreds of coloured lanterns. It was a mild evening, and several pairs of windows were open to the terrace. No doubt couples would be strolling on the lawns later.

He soon found Phoebe and Sally, talking with some of Sally's young friends. Phoebe was looking particularly charming in a pale-blue round gown with an embroidered bodice. He drew her aside and took her dance card.

'Good, may I have the first waltz and the supper dance?'

Smiling, she agreed, and he passed on to greet other people. When it was time to dance with her he found her quieter than usual, and there was a slight frown between her eyes.

'What is it? Has Sally been up to her tricks again?'

She looked startled and hastened to deny it. 'Sally's mother,' she said slowly. 'There was a letter today. She is coming here, in time for Sally's dance.'

'I see. Is Sally pleased?'

'Rather to my surprise, she is delighted. But Sir William doesn't know yet. He has been out all day, and was not back before we came here.'

'And Madame Antoine? It will be rather awkward, I assume, with the dance being at her house.'

Phoebe shook her head. 'I don't know. I've grown to like her, and her husband was at Oxford with Sir William. Perhaps that explains why he is so much in her company.'

'I wasn't aware of that. But has Clara stopped doing up Benton Manor?'

'The letter didn't say. It was very short, just to say she could not miss her daughter's ball. I did wonder whether she means to take Sally back to England.'

In which case, Zachary realized, Phoebe would no longer be needed. He glanced round, saw they were close to doors leading on to the terrace, and swung Phoebe through them.

'Let's walk in the gardens for a while,' he said, tucking her arm through his and leading her down on to the lawn. There were other couples strolling about, so Zachary turned aside into a path bordered by ornamental trees.

When they had gone far enough away for the music to be just a faint echo he stopped, and turned Phoebe to face him.

'Phoebe, my dear, you may find this rather sudden, but believe me, I hold you in great esteem. I have watched how you have dealt with Sally, your patience and common sense, and come to admire you greatly. Will you do me the honour of becoming my wife?'

In the faint glow from the lanterns he could see her face, and the startled expression on it. Then she wrenched her arm away from his grasp and took a couple of hurried steps away from him.

'My lord, I suppose I should be gratified by this proposal, but I cannot help but know your main desire is not for a wife, but for a son to deprive your uncle of his hope of inheriting from you. I'm not a brood mare, so you will understand why I cannot accept your very flattering offer!'

She turned, and before he could prevent her, she was running back along the path towards the house. He swore comprehensively, all the oaths he had learned in Spain and Portugal. He had made a complete mull of that, and it was too late to stop her and try to explain.

11

Phoebe, with tears threatening to overflow, could not endure the thought of returning to the ballroom. It was a warm evening, though only the middle of April, so she turned off the path into a narrower one and came eventually to a small summerhouse. The door was unlocked, and there were cane chairs stacked inside. She set one down just inside the doors, which she pulled to behind her, and breathed deeply. She would not weep! She tried to make herself angry with the earl, but instead of this kept recalling his helpfulness.

How could he have thought she would be content to accept his proposal, when she knew full well the only reason he wanted a wife was to provide a son so that Jonas and his sons could not inherit the title and his fortune. Bleakly she admitted to herself it was a dream she had tried to discourage. She could think of nothing she wanted more, but only if he loved her. Esteem, he'd said. She could not live with a man who merely esteemed her.

Phoebe tried to tell herself there were many marriages where the partners felt no love for one another. They were no less successful. She wondered whether Jane and Reginald had ever felt such emotion, and surprised herself with a giggle. Perhaps she read too many novels where lovers made passionate speeches declaring undying love. Reginald and Jane were both too prosaic and conscious of their dignity to admit to any weakness, and surely they would both regard romantic love as a weakness.

What did they have, she wondered? Jane had a home and income she would not have had as an unmarried daughter of a poor doctor, who treated his poorer patients and never asked them for payment. Reginald had a competent housekeeper to manage his household and children. As a married couple they could mingle in local society to a far greater extent than either could have done alone. It satisfied a need to present themselves and their family to the world as prosperous and successful. Perhaps they had a mutual respect, perhaps a regard for the good qualities of the other. Surely without even that they could not exist in amity. But these were all cold, practical reasons. They had heirs, which was what Zachary wanted most of all.

As a doctor's daughter Phoebe was more knowledgeable than most unmarried girls of the processes of birth and the creation of children. Her father had always answered her questions honestly, and he and her mother had frequently talked about his patients in front of her. She recalled his anger with a man whose wife had died giving birth to their fourteenth child, and his despair that such men were unable to control their appetites for the good of their wives.

Reginald had several sons, but he and Jane continued to produce children. They did not need more, so either they found some satisfaction and pleasure in acts of intimacy, or Reginald was like her father's patient's husband, a man unable to control his appetites. Somehow she could not see Jane meekly submitting to this, but what did she know of the realities of marriage? Would Jane consider it her duty, or did she welcome it? Did she, though Phoebe found this almost impossible to imagine, love Reginald? Phoebe hastily banished a vision of her sister and Reginald naked in bed together. It must happen, but she could scarcely believe it.

Her parents were the only other couple she had known well. She was sure they had been in love. Her mother had been devastated by her father's death. Phoebe sat in the summerhouse, gradually getting colder, recalling the many small acts of kindness unobtrusively performed for her and each other by her parents, the tenderness of their speech, the glances and smiles, the way they seemed to be in accord with one another, able to communicate without words.

She wanted a marriage like that. She wanted warmth and love, not the esteem and cold admiration which was all Zachary Walton had offered. She had been right in her instinctive refusal, she told herself, even though she could think of no man she would rather be married to.

★ ★ ★

Zachary watched Phoebe running away from him and was furious at his ineptitude. For a moment he contemplated going after her and trying to explain, but the possession of sisters had taught him that explanations to a woman who was angry were pointless. When she was calmer, perhaps he would be able to talk to her. She could not leave the ball until Sir William and Sally did, and she could not stay in the gardens all evening. She had promised him the supper dance, and maybe he would be able to talk to her then.

After a while he went back to the ballroom, but found he was unable to chat to his partners with his usual ease. One of them, a young married woman he had known since they were children, commented on his abstraction, but fortunately put it down to worry about the prospect of war. He could not tell her that all thoughts of Bonaparte and what was coming had been driven completely out of his head.

He had, he knew, offered for Phoebe because he admired her and thought her suitable to be his wife and the mother of his sons. When she rejected him so contemptuously he had suddenly seen how disparaging it must have seemed to her, to be asked solely because he needed a wife and she was available. For a moment he felt a surge of anger. Why did all females want to hear love speeches? Marriage was not something to be entered into just because two people thought they were experiencing some amorous sentiment, a feeling which would, sooner or later, be lost to them.

Then he began to wonder why he had never before wanted to offer for any of the many supremely suitable damsels who had been thrust into his notice by ambitious mamas. Was his determination to marry now solely due to his desire to frustrate Jonas's ambitions? If it was, there were girls enough here in Brussels who would, in the eyes of the polite world, be far more suitable than Phoebe Kingston.

He experienced a sense of surprise. Could it be that, unaware of it, he had come to regard Phoebe with something more than the esteem he had offered her? Was he in love with her?

The notion was startling. After a few youthful occasions when he had considered he was in love, a feeling which had lasted no more than a few weeks, he had never again experienced the same emotions. He had always said farewell and never looked back, or regretted the loss of his temporary mistresses. This needed serious thought, but he could not concentrate while dancing. He would suggest to Phoebe that they sat out the supper dance and talked.

Phoebe was nowhere to be found. During the whole of the supper dance, and while the other guests were eating, he searched the house, and then went outside to look in the gardens. It was cold now, and everyone had retreated indoors. As he explored the paths through a dense shrubbery he happened to glance back at the house and saw a slender figure slipping through the doors into the ballroom. He ran across the intervening lawn and entered the room just as the orchestra struck up for the next dance. He saw Phoebe standing nearby, but at that moment her partner appeared and led her on to the floor.

Zachary, mindful of his obligations, had to seek his own partner, and for the rest of the evening he had no more opportunity of exchanging a word with Phoebe.

★ ★ ★

It was the day before Sally's ball when Lady Benton arrived in Brussels. Sir William was in the drawing-room with the girls before dinner when the footman appeared, looking rather puzzled.

'Sir William, Lady Benton is here.'

He was pushed gently aside as Lady Benton, still wearing her travelling cloak, came into the room. 'Thank you. Can you see to my luggage, please, and tell the coachman where he may stable the horses.'

She had not finished before Sally, with a glad cry, was across the room and throwing herself into her mother's arms. Sir William, rather slower, stood looking at them and smiling.

Phoebe was puzzled. Sally and her mother had not appeared to be on affectionate terms when she had stayed with them at Benton Manor, and Lady Benton had been only too glad to send Sally away.

'How pleasant to have you here for Sally's ball,' Sir William said.

Lady Benton put Sally aside and went to her husband, who kissed her on the cheek.

'I have been hearing such terrible things about Bonaparte, I had to come and be sure you were both safe. Besides, Mr Cowper is being difficult; he will not listen to what I want him to do, and all the building is at a standstill until I can find another architect. It is so convenient that I can come and supervise the ball.'

'You don't need to do anything, Phoebe has done it, with Madame Antoine,' Sally said.

She did not appear discomposed at the evidence of her mother's priorities, Phoebe thought, suppressing a smile. She was just delighted to see her mother. Perhaps their separation for the past three months had made both of them more affectionate.

Lady Benton nodded. 'Phoebe, Sally's letters have all been full of praise for you. Thank you for your care of her. Now, can I be shown my room, and I will be ready to join you for dinner, if you will excuse my not changing. I would not wish to delay you. Are you going out this evening?'

'Let me show you the way,' Sir William said, and led her out of the room.

There were no spare bedrooms, Phoebe reflected. Would Sir William and his wife be forced to share one? She had never been into his room, but she knew there was a small dressing room attached. Perhaps he would sleep there. Then she gave up speculating. The state of their marriage was none of her business, and Sally was bubbling over with excitement that her mother had arrived so unexpectedly. She had to listen to her.

During the evening Phoebe began to wonder whether her own position was now redundant. If Lady Benton stayed, she was no longer needed as Sally's companion. Would they send her home? She did not in the least wish to go, but neither did she wish to meet the earl again.

Lady Benton had appeared worried, and during dinner mentioned her wish to take Sally home immediately after the ball, but Sir William had shaken his head.

'I thought the idea of this ball was to introduce her to Society, and get her betrothed,' he said bluntly. 'It won't serve its purpose if you whisk her away before any of the young men can come up to scratch. Besides, our fellows will halt Bonaparte long before he gets to Brussels.'

Sally had added her pleas to be allowed to remain, and her mother, shrugging, promised to wait and see.

'But if that monster crosses the border, we'll have to go.'

★ ★ ★

Zachary was uncharacteristically indecisive. Several times he had been about to call on Phoebe and try to explain his ineptitude when he had proposed to her. The trouble was, he was unable to explain it to himself. He wanted to marry her. She would be an ideal wife for him. But how could he make her understand that?

He didn't know whether he loved her or not. He didn't think he knew what love was. Perhaps it was a desire to be always in the company of someone. Perhaps it was a need to care for them, look after them, ensure no harm came to them. He had never felt this for anyone else. Girls who were more beautiful, better born, wealthier, had set their caps at him in the past, and he had felt nothing. How could he explain this to Phoebe and make her believe him?

He had not solved the problem when the day of Sally's ball arrived. He contemplated not going. There was quite sufficient work to be done, as the duke strove to collect an army capable of opposing Bonaparte. He needed more men, particularly experienced soldiers.

The equipment he had was inadequate, few of the staff officers he knew and depended on were available. Others he did not know or want had been appointed without his knowledge by the Duke of York.

In the end Zachary had to attend the ball. His need to see Phoebe again overrode every other consideration. He delayed until he could be certain most of the guests were there, for he did not wish to be put in the position of soliciting a dance from Phoebe and being refused. He would content himself with watching her, and trying to judge from her demeanour towards him whether he could talk to her soon, explain himself, or whether he had more work to do to regain her confidence.

As he entered the house he was startled to see Sir William waiting to receive guests, flanked by Madame Antoine and Lady Benton. He had not known of the latter's arrival in Brussels.

'My dear Wrekin,' Sir William greeted him. 'You know my wife, of course. She decided to come to Brussels after all for Sally's ball.'

Zachary bowed to both ladies. 'I am happy to see you.'

'Tell me, my lord, how dangerous is it to remain here? I want to take Sally home if there is any danger of Napoleon attacking

Brussels, but I realize it would be a pity now she has made an official debut.'

'Lady Benton, you can be sure the army will protect Brussels. The duke is confident, and he has always prevailed before.'

'In the end, yes, but he had to retreat from Spain before he finally won. And he and Bonaparte have never met in battle, I think?'

'This time the whole of Europe is with us, we are not fighting alone.'

'But where are all these others? My husband tells me all you have are untried boys, and Dutch and Belgian boys at that. They cannot compare with good English troops.'

Zachary suppressed a smile. Her stout support for English troops might be admirable and patriotic, and he had no wish to disillusion her. They did not have the best regiments here in Flanders.

'There are more of the veterans coming every day,' he said, 'and the Prussians are joining us.'

She had to turn away then to greet another late arrival, and Zachary made his way into the ballroom. He stood for a while watching the dancers, and soon spotted Phoebe dancing with one of the young cavalry officers he had seen occasionally with Sally. She was smiling at him, and Zachary's heart turned over. He wanted to stride on to the floor and drag her away from the man. She appeared the same as ever, until he looked closer and saw a slight frown between her eyes. Then she glanced across and saw him. Although she turned away immediately a deep flush stained her cheeks.

The dance came to an end and Phoebe, with a quick glance towards him, urged her partner to walk in the opposite direction. Zachary gritted his teeth. Now he knew. She would not willingly speak to him. Should he corner her here in a very public place, where she could not escape him, and force her, out of politeness, to speak to him? No sooner had he thought of this he knew he could not do it to her. He had no wish to cause her any distress. His very presence was making her nervous, and he suspected she would be on tenterhooks all the time, waiting for him to approach her.

At that moment he saw Sally approaching, with Sir Henry ffoulkes, and he went to meet her.

'Sally, I hope you are enjoying your ball. It seems to be going well. I was pleased to see your mother here.'

Sally beamed at him. 'It was wonderful of her to come, but I think she wants to take me home if that horrid Napoleon starts to fight.

Please will you tell her it's quite safe to remain here? I don't wish to go home.'

'I have already tried to persuade her there is no need. Sally, I really only came to wish you well. I must go back to the embassy, there are letters I need to write. Please thank your parents, and Madame Antoine. And will you explain to Phoebe I have to leave? Give her my best wishes. I have not been able to speak to her.'

'What a shame. Yes, I will tell her, and thank you for coming, even if it was for just a short time.'

★ ★ ★

Phoebe had spent many sleepless hours wondering how she would feel when she saw the earl again. She had no doubt they would meet. The English community in Brussels were eager to make the most of their time, and every day there were balls and receptions, and now the weather was getting warmer, picnics and garden parties. They were bound to meet at some of these.

She had wondered whether he would come to Sally's ball. Part of her dreaded the meeting, which would be in public, but another part of her longed to see him again. Even though she had rejected his proposal,

250

and in a manner which would have disgusted him, the thought of never again seeing him was insupportable.

When she did see him, looking across the crowded dance floor at her, she had read contempt in his expression. Of course, her graceless refusal of his proposal would have angered him. From what Lady Drayton had said he had never offered for a girl, despite the urgings of his sisters that he marry. Then he had offered for her, a penniless companion, far below him socially, and with no beauty or other talents to commend her, and been rejected, which would have been like a blow in the face. He could marry anyone, and she had not only turned him down, but been astonishingly rude in the manner of it.

When the dance ended she hurried her partner off the floor and tried to lose herself in the crowd. Would he approach her? She did not think so, but just in case he did intend to try to speak to her, she meant to make it as difficult as possible. She did not know how she could face him. At the very least she would be stammering and speechless, and she feared she might even burst into tears.

She greeted her next partner with flattering enthusiasm, and only relaxed when they were safely established in the set. The earl could not interrupt this. As they danced she tried to see where he was, but he had moved and she could not find him. Was he lying in wait for her? In her nervousness she paid little attention to the dance, and had to be called back when she moved the wrong way.

Trying to laugh at her mistake, she gave up attempting to see where the earl was, and finished the dance in a state of fatalism. If he sought her out, and she created some kind of disturbance, it would be his fault.

Her partner, another of the young soldiers, led her off the floor at the end of the dance, making painstaking conversation. Phoebe heard nothing, and jumped as someone touched her arm.

'Phoebe, it's only me.'

It was Sally, and Phoebe's heartbeat slowed back to normal.

'Are you enjoying the ball?' she asked, but her voice was hoarse and the words were barely recognizable.

'It's wonderful. Are you all right? Your voice sounds odd. You are not taking a cold?'

Phoebe cleared her throat. 'No, of course not. It's just that I need a drink.'

'Then come and let's find one. Oh, the earl said to give you his best wishes. He has to go back to write more tedious letters.'

Phoebe took a deep breath. 'He has left?'

'Yes, a little while ago, soon after the last dance started. He was only here for a few minutes.'

She was safe, she would not have to see him, perhaps speak to him, this evening. Phoebe knew she ought to feel thankful, but for just a few moments she felt deserted, lost. That was ridiculous, she scolded herself, and for the rest of the evening did her utmost to appear cheerful and enjoying herself.

She was heartily glad when the ball was over, and they were able to go home. When Sally wanted to come into her room to discuss the ball, she pleaded exhaustion and sent the girl away. She was tired, but sleep would not come. A tiny, insistent voice kept asking her if she had not been incredibly stupid to reject the earl. He might not love her, but she would have been his wife, and would have had the opportunity of making him love her.

★ ★ ★

Phoebe was sitting with Sally and her mother in the drawing-room the following morning, discussing the ball. Lady Benton was full of praise for the way she and Madam Antoine had organized it.

253

'So sad that her husband died so soon after their marriage,' Lady Benton said. 'They were so in love.'

Phoebe was puzzled. Brussels society had been convinced Sir William and Madame Antoine were lovers, yet here was his wife on apparently friendly terms with the lady. Was this the way civilized people behaved? If it was, she heartily disapproved.

Sally, who must have heard the rumours, was looking puzzled. 'You knew her before, Mama?'

'We were at the same school in Bath for several years. When your father came here I asked him to meet her.'

'I see.' Sally, who was holding a piece of embroidery on her lap, suddenly put it down and looked at the clock. 'Is that the time? Is the clock fast?'

She jumped up and went to the window, standing there looking down into the street. She had a handkerchief in her hand and was twisting it mercilessly. Phoebe wondered what was disturbing her.

Sally wandered back to her chair and picked up the embroidery, but did not make any attempt to sew. 'I'm sure that clock has stopped,' she said.

At that moment they heard the knocker on the front door, and Sally stood up, the embroidery dropping unheeded to the floor.

'Sally, what is it? You are so restless this morning,' Lady Benton said. 'Pick up that sewing before you tread on it.'

Sally did so and subsided, but kept glancing at the door. It was ten minutes later when the footman appeared and asked Lady Benton if she would please join Sir William in his study.

Lady Benton, eyebrows raised, left the room and Sally once more discarded the embroidery. She leapt up and began pacing the room, twisting her hands together.

'Sally, what on earth is it?' Phoebe asked.

Sally came and sank on to a footstool near Phoebe's chair. 'It's Henry,' she said.

'Sir Henry ffoulkes?'

'Yes. He's come to ask Papa if we can be betrothed. Oh, Phoebe, I'm so nervous! What if Papa refuses him? I shall die, I know I will!'

'Of course you won't. Why should your father refuse him? He's a suitable match, and your parents want you to be betrothed,' Phoebe said, taking Sally's hand in hers. They were longing to get her off their hands, she thought, but refrained from saying so.

It was another twenty minutes before Sally's parents entered the room, followed by a grinning Sir Henry and the footman carrying a tray with a bottle of champagne and glasses.

'Papa?'

Sally could scarcely speak for excitement. She was beaming, and there were tears in her eyes.

'My dear, Sir Henry has asked me for your hand, and I have accepted him, providing you are agreeable,' Sir William said, his voice solemn.

Phoebe almost laughed. As if there could be any doubt Sally would accept him. Since the pair had met they had been close. Sally knew several soldiers, but had from the start shown her preference for Sir Henry.

'Yes. Of course. Oh, Henry! Mama!' Sally cast herself into her mother's arms. 'When can we be married?'

'Steady, my child,' Lady Benton said, and Phoebe detected a note of complacency in her voice. 'You must be married at home, of course, and there will be much to arrange. We cannot make plans until this business with Bonaparte is settled. Perhaps next year? A spring wedding would be pretty, and by then my building work will be completed.'

'A whole year?' Sally was aghast. 'Mama!'

'You are both young,' Lady Benton began, and Sally interrupted.

'But I know I won't change my mind!'

She had soon forgotten George Cowper, Phoebe thought, and then chided herself for the thought. Sally had used him as a means of rebellion. Her affection for Sir Henry, and his for her, were genuine. They seemed deep in love, and Phoebe felt considerable jealousy of her young friend.

'Of course not,' Lady Benton said, 'I am not suggesting that. You need to buy your trousseau, and there are a hundred other things to be done.'

'I don't care for that sort of thing. Mama, Henry is a soldier, he could be killed at any moment!'

Sir Henry spoke for the first time. 'We'll stop Boney, Sally, you needn't fear for me. And your mother is right. If you don't have a lovely wedding, you might regret it in the future. We're both young, we can afford to wait.'

He would be so good for Sally, Phoebe thought approvingly. He was sensible, and would control her starts.

'We ought both to return to England at once, I need to finish the house, and you need to plan your trousseau,' Lady Benton said, but Sally looked at her in amazement.

'Mama, I can't! You wouldn't drag me away from Henry now! There's no danger, I promise!'

'If there is any danger, I will make sure Sally goes to England, Lady Benton. It would be hard on us to be separated so soon.'

A sensible young man, Phoebe decided. And it gave her a few more weeks of employment. She felt selfish at the thought, but knew she must begin to consider her own future.

'Let the child stay,' Sir William said, beaming at his daughter. 'We must give a small party for her friends, to announce the betrothal. A week today, a dinner, perhaps?'

'A party, yes, but this dining room is so small, it can only accommodate a dozen people. And we cannot comfortably have more than twenty people in this drawing-room. I would not wish to ask Madame Antoine's help again so soon, so is there a room in a hotel we could hire? It must be soon if I am to return to Benton Manor and the building work.'

'Leave it to me,' Sir William said. 'I agree we cannot ask Madame Antoine to lend us her house again, but she will know of other places.'

* * *

Zachary had more work than he wanted, with all the reports coming from France and elsewhere, but at least it diverted his thoughts from Phoebe and the puzzle of how he was to talk with her and persuade her he really wished to marry her. He excused himself from as many social occasions as he could, while the duke, giving the impression of calm and confidence they all needed, was seen everywhere, attended every party, and gave his own entertainments, mainly a weekly ball.

He was tempted to refuse the invitation to Sally Benton's betrothal party, a grand dinner to be held in one of the large hotels. Then he decided he had to begin seeing Phoebe again, and this would be an ideal opportunity of restoring contact. She could avoid him if she wished, and apart from the unlikely chance they would be seated together at the table, they need not speak. He might, however, be able to convey to her she had no need to fear anything from him.

When he entered the hotel room where the guests were gathering, he immediately saw Phoebe at the far end, talking to an elderly couple he had seen before, but did not know.

She turned away from them after a while and saw him, standing just inside the doorway. He saw her take a deep breath and straighten her shoulders, then, to his surprise, she walked steadily across the room and stopped a yard or so in front of him. Was she afraid to come nearer, he wondered, and gave her what he hoped was a reassuring smile.

'My lord, I want to apologize for my discourtesy. I was rude. It is inevitable that we will meet, Brussels society is comparatively small, and it will not do for us to be always trying to avoid one another.'

He wanted so desperately to take her in his arms and kiss her. She was so gallant. Was this love? Had he, all unaware, fallen in love with her? But he must go carefully. At least this approach by her meant they could meet, and he would perhaps be able to restore their relationship to what it had been, and progress from there. He had a sudden strong conviction that he had to make this girl his wife, she was the only one who would do.

'I have no wish to avoid you, Phoebe. I have always enjoyed your company and would prefer us to remain friends. Is that possible?'

She smiled, and relaxed. 'Thank you. You are kind.'

He was nothing of the sort. He was selfishly considering his own desires, and for the first time since that inept proposal beginning to hope she might, at some later date, accept him.

12

The news in Brussels was contradictory. Phoebe heard Bonaparte had a great army assembled in Paris, then that his support was crumbling. For the rest of April and all of May life went on much as usual. More and more troops arrived and were stationed in a great swathe to the south of Brussels. There was a feverish gaiety at the many entertainments. Sally was deliriously happy whenever Henry could find time to visit her, and miserable when his duties kept him away.

Lady Benton had returned to England, and wrote to say she had secured the services of a really estimable and efficient architect who had assured her all the building alterations would be finished by the end of the year, which would give plenty of time for the new rooms to be decorated before Sally's wedding. Had Sally, she asked, given any thought to bridesmaids? They had few relatives, and no small girl cousins, so perhaps Sally should have some of her friends. She must give urgent thought to this and make sure no one who ought to be included would be offended if not asked.

'I trust this affair with Bonaparte will be over and done with so that everyone will have returned to England,' she concluded.

Phoebe received regular letters from her mother, who seemed resigned to living at Bradshaw Towers, though she said Jane was becoming anxious for Reginald's return. Beatrice wrote more plainly, telling Phoebe she had enjoyed the visit Mrs Kingston had made to Ridgeway Park, and had made her promise to visit again, though Jane had seemed reluctant for her mother to come, and had complained bitterly at the prolonged absence of Dorothy and Hermione. Reginald, it seemed, was permitted his absence since he was doing business, but Jane appeared to resent the idea of his sisters having an enjoyable social life.

Phoebe wished the three Bradshaws would go. Reginald spent a good deal of his time in Ghent, which left his sisters free to visit Phoebe on an almost daily basis. They appeared to think she could introduce them to the more important residents, to whose entertainments they had not been invited. They were especially disgruntled not to obtain tickets to the singer Madame Catalini's benefit.

'But the Queen was there, and Lord Wellington, who was most affable, we heard.

It would have been a wonderful opportunity to meet him,' Dorothy complained.

They also firmly believed she had more information than was available to them.

'But Phoebe, surely Sally's fiancé knows what is happening? He's an officer, and they must have information we don't.'

'If Henry has any private information, it would be his duty to keep it private,' Phoebe said for the tenth time. 'If there are plans for troop movements, they would not want to risk them coming to the ears of the French, would they?'

'But we wouldn't tell the French,' Hermione protested.

Phoebe closed her eyes and prayed for patience. 'Of course not, but you might tell someone else who would, or you might be overheard speaking of it.'

'Well, what about the Earl of Wrekin? He's working very closely with the duke, we hear. Doesn't he tell you anything?'

'No, he does not,' Phoebe said, trying to keep her voice calm. She saw the earl occasionally at balls and picnics, but apart from greeting her and passing the time of day, he did not seek her out. She had not danced with him since that dreadful night when he proposed. Why had she been so vehement in her rejection? If she had been sensible, she could have asked for time to consider, and then she might not have rejected him at all. It was too late now, but she would never cease to regret her hasty temper. If only she had been calmer. Now she thought she would be willing to marry him on any terms. A loveless marriage would be better than the bleak future she faced without him.

★　★　★

Zachary was so busy he had little time for social occasions. Wellington believed the French would probably attack in July, despite the movement of the army northwards. He feared a flanking movement to the west, but was also concerned that Blücher's position was at Namur, to the south-east, and closer to the German border. That left a wide gap due south of Brussels.

When Zachary did see Phoebe he was careful not to appear to put any pressure on her. He never asked her to dance, fearing that any close proximity would make him forget his plan for a steady resumption of their former friendship.

At the end of May, however, he succumbed to his need to be with her and asked her and Sally if they would like to go with him to the review of cavalry.

'Sir William will be going, and I can obtain rooms for you. I shall ride, but you can go by coach.'

'I'd prefer to ride,' Sally protested.

'It's thirty miles away, and the weather is hot. You will be more comfortable in a coach.'

'Henry will be there.' Sally had not seen him for several days, and with the prospect of seeing him she was willing to travel however the earl suggested, so after her token protest she concentrated on planning which gowns to take.

Satisfied with his arrangements, Zachary hoped he would be able to talk to Phoebe in a more relaxed atmosphere than at the balls and Brussels entertainments. He ordered a hamper of food so that they could picnic on the way, and called for them early in the morning.

They joined a veritable procession of coaches and riders. Zachary and Sir William rode alongside, Sir William complaining of the dust thrown up by the carriages in front. When they had gone halfway Zachary turned aside into a narrow lane, and led them to a grove of trees where there was a small clearing.

'We can picnic here,' he said, and Sally exclaimed in delight at the carpet of wild flowers. She jumped down from the coach and began to pick them, making them into a posy which she presented to Phoebe.

'Here, you can pin them to your gown. They are mostly blue, so they look pretty against your lemon gown.'

Phoebe had been spreading out rugs in the shade of the trees for them to sit on, and unpacking the hamper.

'It's years since I did this,' she exclaimed, smiling without reserve at Zachary. 'As a child I used to love riding up into the country near Buxton, but I never had such delicious food as this.'

He knelt beside her and helped take out the food. 'I'll take the wine and put it in the stream to cool,' he suggested.

'A stream? Nearby?'

'Yes, can you hear it?'

She tilted her head to listen, and nodded. 'Oh, how I long to paddle! But I suppose it would be considered unladylike.'

'What's unladylike?' Sally demanded, coming back with another posy she was fastening to her own gown.

'His lordship says there is a stream, and I was longing to paddle.'

'Where? Oh, Phoebe, we must! Do say we can! Papa, you wouldn't mind, would you?'

Sir William had found a fallen branch on which he was sitting. He waved a hand at

Sally. 'Go and be a child, my dear. You will soon be a married lady and much too sedate for such childish pleasures.'

Zachary grinned, and led the way. Somehow he could not imagine Sally married, nor Sir Henry, who was a nice boy, a competent soldier, but in his opinion much too young to take on the burden of a wife.

He caught his thoughts. A wife a burden? He may have thought that a few short weeks ago, but now, too cautious to approach Phoebe again, in case he was rejected a second time, he wanted nothing better than to be married to her.

The stream was shallow, the water clear, and they could see some tiny fish swimming amongst the plants which edged it. While Zachary found a deeper spot to set the bottles of wine, the girls quickly took off their shoes and stockings and, hitching up their skirts, stepped into the water.

It was so cold they shrieked with surprise, and Zachary stood watching them, able to look his fill on Phoebe as she laughed and cautiously stepped further into the stream, then bent down to try and catch the tiny fish.

Soon they came out, unable to stand the cold for long. Phoebe produced a handkerchief and they dried their feet as well as possible, then, as Zachary turned aside to get the bottles of wine, they were able to resume their stockings and shoes, and go back to the picnic.

★   ★   ★

Phoebe and Sally were awed by the display of horsemanship during the review. It was the first time they had seen so many troops together. They had heard various numbers tossed around, so many thousand men stationed here, another ten thousand there, but seeing this exhibition brought home to Phoebe the reality of battle. She could imagine these men charging into the enemy, who would have an equal number, and there her imagination balked at what would come next.

Sally seemed to see only the magnificence of so many beautiful horses and elaborate uniforms. She hadn't realized yet, Phoebe suspected, that Henry would be involved in any fighting, and might be wounded or even killed. The earl, she thought with considerable relief, was a civilian. He would not be involved in the actual fighting. Then she felt selfish. And it was not even as though she had any claim on him.

On the way back to Brussels Sally was full of the glory she had seen, and predicting that when Napoleon was faced with such a magnificent display of military splendour, he would turn round and go back to Paris.

'I don't believe they will fight,' she said more than once.

She grew quieter later that night when her father came in with a sheet of paper which he handed to her. It was, he told them, one of many similar broadsheets which the French had caused to be distributed amongst the Belgians.

Phoebe read it over Sally's shoulder. There was praise for the valiant French troops who had conquered so much in the past, and boasts of what they would soon be doing in Belgium. It was a clear invitation to the Belgians to support Napoleon, with an undisguised threat of what they might expect if they resisted.

'People won't believe this, will they, Papa?'

'Some will, I fear. Several English visitors have already left for Ghent and Bruges. Your brother-in-law, Mr Bradshaw, saw me earlier today, and asked whether they should leave.'

'I hope you told him to,' Phoebe said.

Sir William smiled. He was well aware of Phoebe's dislike of Reginald and his sisters. 'I left it to him. I feel he is the sort of man who will do the opposite just to prove he is independent. He said that if they did go, he would feel it his duty to take you with him, and trusted that Sally and I would not be inconvenienced, losing your services.'

Phoebe stared at him in dismay. 'I certainly don't wish to leave! Oh, I beg your pardon. If you want to send me and Sally home, and have him escort us, of course we will obey you,' she added.

'I can't leave Henry!' Sally cried.

Her father smiled at her. 'I have every confidence in Wellington,' he said, 'and I see no need for you to go. If Phoebe wished to, then of course I would not prevent her, but I take it you have no desire to leave.'

'Of course not.'

'Then I wish you luck if Mr Bradshaw tries to compel you.'

Phoebe went to bed and lay for an hour or more fuming at Reginald's impertinence. She would tell him exactly what she thought of him if he dared to try and order her to leave Sally.

Sir William left the house early, and the girls had scarcely finished breakfast the following day when Reginald appeared and was shown into the drawing-room. Phoebe, shaking her head when Sally offered to stay with her, said she preferred to deal with him alone.

'He'll only try to overawe you, and it will

be upsetting,' she said. 'I'm accustomed to his manner.'

She was accustomed, but she had never before faced Reginald in such a determined, hectoring mood. It took all her resolution to withstand his commands, but in the end he made her so angry she told him exactly what she thought of him.

'I believe you are going home because you are not invited to the more aristocratic affairs,' she said. She had never seen him or his sisters at the Duke of Wellington's parties, or those given by the highest members of the *ton*, and knew that would have offended his dignity.

'You are an impertinent, ungrateful wretch,' he roared at her, his cheeks red with fury. 'I give your mother a home, after your imprudent father leaves you with a pittance — '

'Don't you dare criticize Papa!' Phoebe interrupted. 'He was a far better man than you! He cared for people, but you exploit them, in your mills, and live in luxury off their labour.'

'If that is what you think, you need not come crawling back to us when you do deign to return to England! There's no longer a home for you at Bradshaw Towers, miss!'

'I would not come to your house if I were starving,' Phoebe told him.

He glared at her, then stormed out of the room, and Phoebe collapsed on to a sopha, trembling. She closed her eyes and took a few deep breaths, and found Sally kneeling beside her, anxiously patting her hand.

'Phoebe, that horrible, odious man! How can your sister endure him?'

Phoebe gave an uncertain laugh. 'I've often wondered. Did you hear much?'

Sally chuckled. 'Not at first, but when he began to shout I think everyone in the house heard. I really expected him to start beating you, and then I'd have rushed in to save you.'

'I hope he does not take out his frustration on Mama.'

'Your sister will not let him. But if he does make life so uncomfortable for her she must go to Aunt Beatrice. She would understand. But I've a better idea. We must find you a husband, so that you can offer her a home.'

★   ★   ★

News from France was still unreliable. The duke was unable to send out scouting parties over the border as he had in the Peninsular because of the feelings at home. It would have been described as an act of war by his opponents. Until the French crossed into Belgium he had to rely on inadequate intelligence. Zachary was trying to make sense of contradictory reports which placed Napoleon variously in Paris and towns to the north, when he was shown a report in a French newspaper about the display of force being described as the *Champ de Mai*, reflecting the great assemblies of armies traditional in France for centuries.

This had been on the first day of June, and the main task of the duke was fortifying the defences. The tension amongst those who had the latest news increased, but the ordinary citizens carried on as usual, with balls every night, breakfasts and picnics and rides or drives out to inspect the fortifications. The duke maintained an air of calm assurance, and Zachary thought this was the main reason there was no panic in Brussels.

He had seen little of Phoebe, since he deliberately avoided going to the balls. It was too soon, he told himself, but in his inmost thoughts he knew his reluctance was more to do with a fear she would again reject him. Never before, in any of his dealings with the fair sex, had he doubted his ability to charm them and have them do as he wished.

A week later he decided to take a chance, an innocuous occasion where he could just be friendly. A cricket match had been arranged at Enghien, and when they met while walking in the *parc* one morning he invited Sally and Phoebe to drive there with him to see it.

'Wellington himself plans to go. Have you ever watched a game?'

'I have,' Sally said eagerly. 'I used to watch in the village at home.'

'Papa took me once, when I was quite small,' Phoebe said, 'but I could not understand the rules, they seemed so complicated.'

'It's quite a long drive, two hours or so, but I am sure you will enjoy it. We can take a picnic again, to eat as we watch. The Duke of Richmond is playing, and he is said to be one of the best cricketers in England. I will try to explain the rules as we watch.'

Zachary used his contacts to ensure that Sir Henry ffoulkes would be free of duties that day, so they could take two curricles, Sir Henry driving Sally and Phoebe with him. They would be able to talk. He admonished himself that he must keep to innocuous topics, so as not to frighten her, for it was still too soon to hope she might have changed her mind.

It was a lovely day, the drive was pleasant, and though Phoebe was at first a little dubious about the propriety of allowing Sally to drive so far alone with Sir Henry, the latter kept up with Zachary all the way, and Phoebe ceased to worry.

Phoebe was swift to understand the rules of the game, and watched with interest. 'Do you play?' she asked Zachary.

'I have done, but my duties in the army, and since then at the Foreign Office, have not given me a great deal of opportunity. Though I may try to start a team when I go home, after Napoleon is once more in our hands.'

'Where is your home?'

'In Shropshire, beside the River Severn, a dozen miles from Shrewsbury. It is a lovely part of the country,' he said, and stopped himself from saying more, saying that she would enjoy living there if she married him.

By the time they drove back to Brussels Zachary felt they had reestablished the friendship they had enjoyed before his disastrous proposal, and he felt encouraged to ask if they were attending the ball to be given by the Duchess of Richmond in two days' time.

'Yes, we mean to go,' Phoebe said.

Zachary smiled at her. 'Then may I have the pleasure of a dance with you? The supper dance, if possible?'

Phoebe hesitated, and his heart began to sink. He had been too precipitous. Then she nodded her head.

'I would like that, my lord.'

★ ★ ★

Sally gasped with excitement when they entered the ballroom. It was decorated in gold, crimson and black, and brilliant with the glow of chandeliers. By now they knew most of the important people in Brussels, the diplomats of many countries, the soldiers, both generals and junior officers who belonged to aristocratic families, and the ladies of those same families.

'Our gowns are outshone by the uniforms,' Phoebe said. Sally wore pale pink, while she had on a gown of her favourite primrose yellow. Most of the women wore pastel colours, but the eyes were drawn to the uniforms, especially the scarlet coats and the kilts of the Highlanders.

The Prince of Orange was present, talking excitedly to a group of Belgians, but Phoebe could not see Wellington. The earl was there, in deep conversation with Sir Charles Stuart, the British Ambassador to the Netherlands. As far as she could see, he did not dance at all during the first part of the evening, but moved around the ballroom talking mainly to officers.

It was late when the Duke of Wellington arrived, and he was immediately surrounded by his aides and some of the officers. After he spoke to them they dispersed, and Phoebe, anxiously watching the earl, saw them circulating amongst the officers. These men nodded, and Phoebe realized some of them were quietly slipping away from the ballroom. The prince had gone, and rumours were circulating amongst the guests that the army had been put on the alert. The fighting, so long expected, seemed imminent.

'What is happening?' she demanded of the earl when he came to join her for the supper dance. 'The officers are leaving. Is it true Napoleon is advancing on Brussels? Ought not the duke to be there, preparing to defend us?'

'Phoebe, my dear, there is no need to panic,' he began.

'I'm not panicking, my lord, but it is clear something important is happening, and I am curious.'

'Bonaparte is moving forwards, and has driven the Prussians out of their forward position at Charleroi. They were too far in advance, it would have been impossible to defend it. But now he is on Belgian soil it's war. Come, shall we dance?'

Phoebe shook her head. 'Please, can we sit out? I want you to tell me all you can. Why is the duke here?'

He led her to a sopha at the side of the ballroom. 'I know very little more. The duke has always considered it a strong possibility that the attack would come on the right flank. It's what he would have done. But now Bonaparte is striking at the middle of the defences. He probably hopes to divide us from the Prussians. But they are falling back, and we will concentrate at Quatre Bras, further north. It's a much more defensible position.'

'We didn't ride so far that day, did we?'

'No, it's quite a way beyond the village of Waterloo.'

'I still can't understand why the duke looks so unconcerned. Surely he ought to be with the army, directing them?'

'Just consider who has been at this ball. It is far easier for him to give his instructions to the officers here, where they are concentrated, than do it any other way. You can be sure messages have been sent to those who are not here.'

'Oh, I see. And I suppose those who are

leaving have gone to join their regiments.'

'The ones that are furthest away, yes. Phoebe, I have every confidence that we'll hold them, but promise me, if the French break through and reach Brussels, you will leave. Take Sally home, or go to Beatrice.'

I think he cares, Phoebe thought, and her heart gave a sudden leap. Or perhaps it is just a general wish to see civilians out of the dangerous area.

'Tell me about the Peninsular,' she said. 'You were wounded?'

'Yes, a ball in my shoulder and a gash from a sword on my leg, which took an age to heal. You heard I sold out soon afterwards?'

'Because your brother was killed, and he was your heir. It was necessary. You won't be fighting this time, though, will you?' she asked. 'You're not in the army now.'

He looked thoughtful. 'I was accused of cowardice by some who did not understand.'

Phoebe was indignant. 'You should not heed such ignorant opinions. But the fighting must have been horrific.'

'It was,' he said, and when she persisted, wanting to know more, described some of the battles.

Phoebe was certain he was not going into

the more gory details, but what he said was bad enough, the deprivations, the poor food and worse accommodation, the inadequate medical attention.

'It's better here,' he concluded. 'I should not have told you all of this, it has frightened you.'

'I wanted to know, and I am frightened only for the men who will lose their lives or be injured.'

'While men fight, that will inevitably happen. But look, they are forming the procession into supper. Let us go and join them. Afterwards, I fear I must leave myself.'

★ ★ ★

After supper Sally, subdued, said she wanted to leave. Henry had gone the moment supper was over. Wellington had departed, officers and civilians were leaving, and only a few people remained to dance. On their way home they saw regiments assembling, ready to march out. Some of the men were trying to sleep on the pavements. The noise was louder than during the daytime.

'We won't be able to sleep,' Sally said, a sob in her voice. 'Oh, Phoebe, he will be all right, won't he?'

Phoebe had no difficulty in identifying the

he. She set herself to calm Sally's fears, although she did not totally believe all she said.

'I'm sure Henry will be safe. They don't think Napoleon has as many men as we do. After all, we have the Dutch and the Belgians, as well as the Prussians on our side. The earl told me one of Napoleon's generals has already defected to the Prussians. There may be others who will defect or simply vanish when they see they have no chance of winning.'

They did not attempt to go to bed. With Sir William, they watched through the night at the drawing-room windows. The night was warm, and they had the windows open, so were able to hear the bugles and drums. Once, when a dreadful wailing noise broke out, the girls turned puzzled eyes towards Sir William.

'What on earth is that noise?' Phoebe asked.

'Have you never heard bagpipes before? The Scottish regiments are gathering. Sometimes I think we should send their pipers forward and frighten away the enemy.'

Phoebe managed to laugh, but was not reassured. The reality of what was to come was too horrible. There were noises she identified as hammering, but could not imagine what was happening to cause this. More comprehensible were the neighing of horses and the rumbles of gun carriages. And below it all dogs barked at the uproar, frightened children wept, and distraught women clung to their husbands and sweethearts, delaying what could be their final leavetaking as long as they could.

Heavy eyed, they watched the dawn, saw the regiments march out through the Namur gate, and a few hours later saw the country folk bringing in their produce, just as though it was a normal day.

After breakfast Phoebe and Sally ventured out. It was far too early to expect any news, but they could not settle to anything. All the inhabitants of Brussels seemed to be in the streets, or leaning from their windows, just waiting. It was eerily silent, and when they encountered a mass of troops, officers in black uniforms, which they were told were the Brunswickers, the Belgians just watched, neither cheering nor disapproving.

'Are they supporting the French?' Sally, subdued, whispered.

'I expect some are,' Phoebe replied. 'Not everyone suffered under their occupation.'

At Sally's suggestion they tried to find the earl. He was not at the embassy, and despite Phoebe's reluctance she permitted Sally to go to enquire at his lodgings.

'The gentleman left in the middle of the night, gone with the soldiers,' the landlady told them.

Phoebe went pale and clutched at Sally's hand. 'But he's not a soldier,' she protested.

His valet then appeared behind the landlady. 'Miss Kingston? Yes, he left with the duke early this morning. Said he couldn't endure to wait here for news, and he might be able to help. The duke has few enough men on his staff he can depend on. I've been with his lordship for years, his batman I was in Spain, and knowing him, I'm sure he'll be in the thick of it.'

13

Phoebe and Sally waited anxiously all day for news. When they heard cheering in the streets they went out to discover rumours that the French had been defeated. Soon afterwards they were being told the French had won and a great victory dinner was being prepared for when Napoleon entered Brussels. This report was believed when some Netherlands soldiers came straggling in, along with some Brunswickers, saying all was lost. The wounded were being brought in on carts, but had little to tell. To keep themselves occupied Sally and Phoebe began to help tend them in the makeshift hospitals.

For some time the distant sound of guns could be heard, and in the evening both girls joined the crowds on the city ramparts, listening in fear and desperate for reliable news. It was while they were there that they heard the rumour of the duke's narrow escape.

'It were when them damned Netherlanders took fright,' a man who had had his arm broken and who had been sent back to Brussels, told them. 'A right mess they left behind 'em, and the duke, bless him, was stuck in the front. He 'ad to flee for 'is life, and I saw it with me own eyes. There was some of them Scots, Gordon Highlanders — they may dress in skirts like women, but by gum, can't they fight — well, they was lyin' in a ditch, bayonets out, when Nosey went flyin' up to 'em, yellin' at 'em to lie down, and blow me, 'e sailed right over 'em. Blimey, that's a great 'orse 'e's got!'

Phoebe and Sally snatched a few hours to sleep, but there were so many wounded being brought in and they were so busy tending them that they could not spare the time to disentangle the contradictory rumours flooding the city. Messages came to ladies whose loved ones were fighting, and the news soon spread, but the general fear was that Napoleon was advancing. Sir William fared little better, but he did get some news from the embassy. He told them, when he found them and insisted they went back to the house for a meal, that the Charleroi road was blocked with carts full of wounded, along with others which had broken down and were blocking the road.

'They are saying we are retreating, that Napoleon has won and will soon be here,' Sally said as they sat down to a meal of cold meat and cheese.

'The duke held off the French at Quatre Bras,' Sir William said, 'but it's not a good position to hold. Napoleon might swing round by the side and get between him and Brussels. He's retreating so that he can make a stand at a better place. He's known for those sort of tactics.'

This was little comfort for Phoebe and Sally, anxious for news of the earl and Sir Henry. Every time she approached another wounded man Phoebe expected to see the earl's face looking up at her.

When they went back to the wounded, there was a strong wind blowing, and suddenly the sky went dark as huge thunder clouds swept in from the north-west, putting the whole city in shadow and sweeping southwards over the Forest of Soigny.

The first enormously loud clap of thunder made Phoebe jump, and almost immediately there was a torrential downpour which soaked her to the skin in seconds. Many of the wounded were lying in the open, on the grass of the *parc* and in other open spaces, even on the pavements, and within minutes they appeared to be lying in a lake, so heavy was the downpour.

Sally was almost crying with weariness and anxiety. 'We can't leave these poor men here,' she said. 'Look, some of them can walk, we must give them shelter. Let's take them home, and they can lie down in the drawing-room.'

Other people were opening up their houses, churches were being turned into temporary hospitals, and the less badly injured were helping their comrades to move, but by the time Sally and Phoebe had taken a score of injured men back to the house they were all soaking wet. Annie and Jeanette found sheets, towels and blankets, and the men were able to strip off their saturated clothing and wrap themselves in something dry. Cook had made a huge cauldron of soup, and baked dozens of rolls. The men, some of whom had not eaten since the previous day, ate the bread and drank the soup gratefully.

Phoebe was concerned they had very few mattresses, but the men were cheerful, telling her they were used to sleeping on the ground, and lying on a dry carpet was a luxury. The dining room was also commandeered, and they fetched in a dozen more of the wounded.

Sally was desperate to go out and try to find news of Sir Henry, but the continuing downpour and Phoebe's demand that she stayed to help those wounded they had in the house made her abandon the idea.

'There are thousands of men out there, your chances of finding him are so small,

you'll be wasting your time and energy,'
Phoebe told her. 'These men need you now.'

★ ★ ★

Zachary, taking messages, wishing he had a
more active role in the fighting, was certain
that if Wellington had been able to use more
of his Peninsula veterans, the battle at Quatre
Bras would have been the final one. The
Dutch and Belgian regiments, untried and
inexperienced boys, were of little use, and he
was not surprised when their collective nerve
broke.

The Prussians, they eventually learned, had
retreated to Wavre, so their own retreat on the
day after the battle, to the ridge at
Mont-Saint-Jean, was essential, or they would
have been dangerously exposed. Wellington,
as he knew from his own days in the army,
was a master of tactical retreats. The duke
liked to choose the ground on which to fight,
and the gently undulating ground, with the
Forest of Soigny at the rear, gave ample cover
for him to dispose his troops out of sight
until the critical moment when they were
employed.

The storm which engulfed them dangerously hampered the retreat. The roads to
Brussels were full of the wounded, some

walking, helping one another along, some in carts, others lying across the backs of horses. The great paved *chaussée* which was the road from Brussels to Charleroi was passable, though the narrow road through the village of Genappe was a bottleneck. The fields to either side were seas of mud, impeding men and horses, and were impossible for any sort of wheeled vehicles.

Soaked to the skin, Zachary managed to find a spot against the side of a cottage where he could tether his horse, letting it graze on a tiny patch of grass, and lean against the wall where he spent a wet, uncomfortable night, dozing occasionally, but more often staring into the darkness and listening for any sounds that could indicate movement. Messengers were still coming, and he knew the duke would have no more than a couple of hours of sleep. The soldiers had to bed down where they could, in the mud or in the drenched corn, and would have a miserable night of it, not a good preparation for battle the next day, which would decide whether Napoleon's bid to recapture Belgium would be foiled, or whether another long period of warfare was in prospect.

Frequently his thoughts turned to Phoebe. He hoped they had recovered a normal friendship at the ball, which seemed so long ago, but was just two days. Perhaps he should have told her he meant to offer his services to the duke. But if he survived — he caught himself, he must survive — he would be able to tell her he wanted her for herself, not for any heirs she might give him. For the first time in his adult life, and he found the notion somewhat amazing, he was in love.

★ ★ ★

All that Sunday rumours flooded Brussels. The sound of gunfire could be heard, and everyone knew the decisive battle was taking place. Phoebe, going out late in the morning to try and find reliable news, met the Bradshaws, struggling to carry several bundles, returning to their hotel.

'What are you doing?' she asked.

Hermione, through her tears, explained.

'We were hoping to get on a barge to Antwerp, but no one is allowed, they are using all the carts and barges to move the wounded away from Brussels. We'll all be killed in our beds!'

There was nothing Phoebe could say, and she left them as they were demanding that she ask her important friends to help them escape.

On the next street she found a group of

women, laden with baskets and bundles, struggling to make their way against the crowds of wounded coming into Brussels. She followed them for a while since they seemed to have a purpose.

She could hear them asking for news of their husbands, especially eagerly when they saw particular uniforms. The answers were always negative, so they hunched their shoulders and marched on.

'Well, gals, we'll have ter go all the way till we can see the fighting,' she heard one of them say. 'They'll need some o' this food an' a pint of ale.'

Thank goodness Sally had not been with her and heard them, or she would have been off to look for Sir Henry.

She stepped to one side to permit a ragged group of soldiers, leading a horse on which a man in the uniform of a French officer was tied with ropes. He had his helmet pushed as far down over his face as possible, and it was impossible to see his features.

'It's Boney himself!'

'Can't be, the French are winning.'

That seemed to be the prevailing opinion, and as Phoebe went back to the house, she saw that people were hurriedly closing their windows and barring the shutters, as panic spread.

There was nothing she could do, and she must concentrate on looking after the wounded they had taken in. She would have to wait, much as the prospect appalled her. At least she and the earl had parted on better terms at the ball. Was it less than three days ago? It seemed like three years.

She was exhausted but unable to sleep. Sir William had sent her and Sally to bed, saying Annie and Jeanette could take over what nursing needed to be done during the night.

'We'll hear of victory in the morning,' he told them.

'How can you be sure?' Sally demanded, almost in tears. 'Surely the battle is over.'

'And if we had lost don't you think the French would have been pouring into Brussels by now?'

Phoebe shivered. She'd ridden along that road when it was clear, but now, with all the wounded and the carts blocking the way, it could take hours for anyone to ride in. If the battle had lasted all day, there might still be time for the victorious French to arrive.

She sat by her window, which overlooked the street, trying to tell herself not to be foolish. If the allies had lost, news would have reached them by now.

It was an hour later, and she was half asleep, when she heard the sound of cheering.

Looking out of the window she saw several men on horseback clattering down the street.

'Boney's beat!' they cried.

They were so completely covered with mud it was impossible to distinguish any uniforms, but the voices were English.

'Boney's on the run! But we'll soon catch him!'

Phoebe sighed. Tomorrow she would know the earl's fate, but somehow she thought she would have known had he been killed. Something in her heart would have broken. She went to bed at last, and slept peacefully for the first time in days.

★ ★ ★

Sally was standing by the window, when she gasped, turned, and ran out of the room. Phoebe, who was changing the bandage on a soldier's arm, which had been badly cut by a sabre, glanced up and raised her eyebrows. Sally had risen that morning with deep shadows under her eyes, and was annoying Phoebe by asking every few minutes when Henry would be coming back to Brussels.

Phoebe tucked in the end of the bandage, a strip torn from a bedsheet, and, as there were no more urgent tasks to be attended to, went to look out of the window.

Sally was clinging to the black mane of a tired-looking grey horse, his colour barely recognizable since he was covered in mud. The man riding him was equally begrimed, but he had washed his face, and Phoebe saw it was one of Sir Henry's friends. He shook his head, and as Sally let go the horse plodded on. Sally turned and ran back into the house.

Phoebe went to meet her on the stairs. She was wild-eyed, struggling to keep the tears from falling.

'Sally, what is it?'

'Peter doesn't know what's happened to Henry. He thinks he was thrown from his horse, but he said it was all so confused, it was almost dark, and there was smoke from the guns all over the area, and they couldn't find him afterwards. Phoebe, I have to go and look for him!'

Phoebe was aghast. This was a mad scheme. 'You'd never find him! There were tens of thousands of soldiers, the battlefield must have stretched for miles!'

'Peter says it happened near an inn. It was in the final charge, when the French were retreating. An inn called La Belle Alliance. Phoebe, if I can find my way there I know I'll find him!'

'Your father won't permit you to go,' she

294

tried, holding out her arms to prevent Sally pushing past.

'He's not here, he went to the embassy.'

'But look at the crowd of people coming towards Brussels. You'll never get through them.'

'I'll ride, and then I can bring Henry back. Oh, do stop arguing, Phoebe, and let me get past.'

'A girl alone, you could be in all sorts of danger.'

'I'll wear my breeches, they'll think I'm a boy.'

Phoebe frowned. 'But I took them away from you.'

Sally tried once more to push past. 'I had another pair,' she almost screamed. 'Phoebe, I'm going, and you won't stop me.'

Phoebe knew that only force could prevent Sally from carrying out her plan. She could hardly lock her into her room, or tie her up. She made up her mind suddenly.

'Then I'll wear the other pair and we'll both go.'

★ ★ ★

Zachary's weary horse stumbled slightly and the earl, who had been riding with a loose rein, hurriedly pulled him up. Though they

295

had been able to sleep the night after the battle, in the shelter of a small copse, the horse tethered to a low branch and Zachary rolled in his greatcoat and his back against a tree trunk, their exertions during almost twelve hours of battle had exhausted them. He hadn't woken until midday, and then only because he had felt a hand trying to roll him out of the coat. When the would-be robber saw he was not dealing with a corpse, he had fled, and Zachary had been too stiff to follow. It was a scorching hot day, which made the stench of smoke and gunpowder, blood and corpses, almost intolerable.

The duke had fired off instructions to all sections of the army, and sent his aides galloping across the battlefield to deliver them. Zachary, though not officially attached to the staff, had been used, and as the day wore on he was needed even more, as one after another the aides were killed or wounded.

Zachary would have dismounted to help the horse, but he was barely able to walk and knew it would lessen their chances of reaching Brussels on their own. There were far too many seriously wounded men being carried in on carts for him to hope to join them. His thigh had been grazed by a bullet towards the end of the fighting, and was still oozing blood. It was red hot, and after the night spent on the wet ground, with no treatment apart from his cravat being bound round his leg, it had stiffened.

He reached the small village of Waterloo, where the duke had his headquarters, and was wondering whether he might be needed. The door of the inn was open, and as Zachary paused one of the staff emerged.

'Wrekin, good to see you're still with us. You're late,' he commented. 'You're wounded?'

'Not badly. Are there any orders?'

'No, the old man left here at dawn, he'll be harrying those in Brussels by now.'

Zachary nodded, and went on. A hundred yards further his attention was drawn to two youths, because they were well-dressed, clean, riding beautifully groomed and slightly frisky horses with bulging saddle-bags, and leading another riderless horse. Then his eyes widened in disbelief. Was he hallucinating? The youth wearing a dark-blue coat rather too large for his slight frame was no youth. Surely it was Phoebe Kingston.

★ ★ ★

Phoebe saw him at the same moment, and felt a great weight lift from her. He was alive. He looked tired and grey, was covered in mud, but he was alive. She turned her horse, the one Sir William normally rode, and halted beside him. Sally rode up on his far side, looking rather pale as she saw the state he was in.

'Zachary!' Then she realized she had, for the first time, used his name, and blushed. 'I mean, my lord. Oh, how thankful I am to see you!'

'Phoebe? And Sally. Are you mad? What the devil are you doing here, dressed like that?'

Phoebe was silent, but Sally burst into speech.

'Henry didn't come back; I'm going to find him, and Phoebe insisted on coming with me.'

'We know roughly where he might be,' Phoebe explained. 'A friend said he was probably unhorsed, in the final charge, near the inn called La Belle Alliance. We went there when we rode out, weeks ago.'

Zachary nodded. 'It was Bonaparte's headquarters. But do you have any notion of what the field is like?'

Phoebe swallowed. 'I think so. We heard that thousands have been killed. And — and there won't have been time to bury them, will there? Besides, we have seen men along the *chaussée* who have died trying to get to Brussels. You need not be afraid we will faint, whatever the horrors.'

'You can't go there, child!'

'You can't stop us,' Sally said, and urged her horse on.

Zachary caught her reins and forced her to halt. 'Not by force, I agree. Will you allow me to go and look for you?'

Phoebe and Sally spoke at the same time.

'No, I'm going, I'm betrothed to him.'

'You look ill, and you must be terribly tired. We heard how long the battle lasted, and even though you are not now in the army you have obviously been involved.' She looked at the blood on his breeches. 'You've been wounded, too. You need rest and proper attention, not more riding in this hot sun.'

'I am coming with you.'

He turned his horse and the three of them rode on, not speaking. Though she guessed what an effort it must be for him, Phoebe was selfishly glad to have his company. If they found Sir Henry either dead or badly wounded she did not feel capable of dealing with Sally, who would be distraught and hysterical.

When they rode up on to the ridge and she saw the devastation spread out for as far as she could see it was all Phoebe could do to keep moving. There were thousands of bodies, horses as well as men, scattered like broken toys in the mud and trampled corn. There were abandoned gun carriages and their deadly cargo, and the smell was so overpowering she gagged and clapped her hand over her mouth. Some buildings in front were still smoking, and there was a shimmering haze over the whole. As they moved closer she could hear weak calls for help. She wanted to stop, but the sheer scale of the task of helping these unfortunates defeated her. They had come to try and find Henry, and she must think only of that.

'This way, there is a road,' the earl said quietly.

'Look, there are people helping,' Sally said, and indeed there were some men moving amongst the carnage. There were women too, weeping and calling as they searched for husbands.

Then Phoebe gasped in shock. 'That man, he is robbing them, taking off rings and searching in pockets, not trying to help at all!'

'What is that one doing?' Sally asked, as they passed close to a man bending over another corpse. 'He looks — oh, no! He's pulling teeth, like a dentist! How, Why?'

'They will sell them, for the artificial teeth some people now want,' Zachary told her. 'Come, you can see La Belle Alliance over there. Concentrate on looking for your Henry. There is nothing you can do here to help.'

★ ★ ★

They found him, three hours later. The ground was littered with debris as well as bodies, discarded weapons, swords and guns, bayonets and pistols, helmets, knapsacks, and scabbards. Playing cards, the torn leaves of books, all sorts of paper, littered the ground or blew about. A sheet of paper fluttered on to Phoebe's saddle pommel, and instinctively she grabbed it and glanced down. It was the beginning of a letter: *My darling Minnie, we will be starting soon, but I will write further when I have a moment.* The edges of the paper were streaked with brown, dried blood, and tears came to her eyes as she thought Minnie would never receive another letter from her lover.

Henry was sitting propped against the body of a dead grey horse, rhythmically rocking to and fro. There was a livid bruise on his face and one eye was closed and puffy. His breeches were torn and stiff with dried blood. He cradled his right arm against his chest, and was moaning. As Sally flung herself from the saddle and ran to him, Phoebe heard him faintly asking for water.

She dismounted more slowly, and began to unpack the saddle-bags she had insisted on bringing. First she took out a bottle of water and went to offer it to Henry.

'Hold it for him, Sally,' she ordered, when she saw Henry was too weak to do so. 'And be careful of his arm, I think it may be broken. Don't let him have too much, I've some brandy here too.'

Zachary, having tethered the horses to a nearby tree, limped across to them. Kneeling down beside Henry he gently explored the leg beneath the torn breeches.

'I think there's a bullet lodged in his calf. It would be better to get him to a doctor than try to deal with it ourselves. Can you help me lift him on to that horse you so sensibly brought?'

It was a struggle, for Henry fainted as they moved him and was incapable of helping himself, and Zachary had little strength left, but at last they had him sitting in the saddle, strapped on to keep him from falling. Then, with Sally and Phoebe riding close beside him to hold him, and Zachary leading the way, they began the long trek back to Brussels.

Phoebe concentrated on the immediate task, shutting her eyes to the horrors around them. As they passed through the village of Waterloo again, she gave the rest of the contents of a saddle-bag to a man Zachary said was a doctor. Henry had been unable to eat the food she had brought, and none of them could face eating. She had also brought bandages and salves, but since they dared not try to deal with Henry's wounds themselves, these could perhaps be better used here.

Sally insisted on taking Henry to their home, and she ruthlessly sent the servants scurrying to fetch a doctor, the mattress from her own bed to put him on, and a host of other things.

'Better not to try and take him upstairs,' Zachary advised, and Sally nodded, opening the door of her father's study and clearing chairs out of the way to make room for the mattress.

'This will do.'

The coachman and footman carried Henry in and laid him down on the mattress. Jeanette then came in almost dragging a Belgian doctor who was grumbling that he could not be spared, and Phoebe stepped outside to where Zachary, exhausted, was leaning against the wall of the house.

'My lord, will you not come in too? You can sleep in my bed, and when you are rested, you can bathe and deal with your wounds. You say they are not serious, but they need to be cleansed and salved.'

Zachary shook his head. 'My rooms are close by, and my valet can do what is necessary. He used to be my batman, and patched me up more than once in the Peninsula. But I don't think I have the energy to mount again, so I'll walk.'

'Lean on me. Hold the saddle with your other arm. We'll get you home.'

She dragged his arm over her shoulder and put her own round his waist. Once or twice she thought he was about to collapse, but after a brief pause he would take a deep breath and start walking again. At last they reached his rooms, she swiftly explained to the valet what had happened, and offered to take the weary horse round to the stables.

'Is there anyone there to tend him?'

'Aye, the groom lives in rooms above.'

'Let me know how he goes on. I must go back now.'

Zachary, leaning heavily on his valet, turned his head and gave her a sweet smile.

'Phoebe, you are wonderful,' he said, before his valet and landlady, who had come out to see what was going on, urged him inside the house.

Henry's arm was broken, and a bullet lodged in his calf, but his other injuries were superficial, bruising and a not very deep gash in his leg. The grumbling doctor removed the bullet, set the broken bones, and left, saying he had more seriously wounded patients to treat. With Sally's devoted care he was soon himself again, weak but lucid, and pathetically grateful to both girls for coming to his rescue.

'I'd have died without you,' he said. 'Many who should have been saved died of exposure or loss of blood.'

'How can he know that?' Phoebe asked, as she and Sally snatched time for a meal, eaten in the kitchen since all their rooms were occupied by wounded men.

'Some of the regiment called to see him this morning. Someone saw us bringing him here and they came to enquire.'

Henry, and everyone else, were wondering what had happened to Napoleon. They heard he had reached Paris three days after the battle, but to a cool reception, and the Prussians, who had arrived on the field late but so opportunely, were in hot pursuit.

'This time he will be sent much further away than Elba,' Henry predicted, 'but we have to catch him first.'

'He can't escape, he's surrounded,' Sally reassured him. She had become avid for all the news, in between her ministrations to Henry.

The only news Phoebe wanted was how the earl was progressing. He had been exhausted, but had made light of his wound, and surely, she thought, he must be able to get about by now. She told herself he would be busy at his work, but surely he could have found time, if not to come and see her, to ask how Henry was. Unless, and the thought terrified her, he had been sent somewhere with despatches. If so, she might never see him again.

'Papa says we must leave Brussels as soon as Henry is fit to travel,' Sally said a week later. 'He is afraid of contamination, for there are so many dead bodies still lying in the streets, and he believes the pestilence can be spread through the air.'

'There is certainly a strong smell,' Phoebe agreed. She had been deputed to do the marketing for the household, while the maids took over most of the nursing, so she had seen the chaos and horror in the streets. 'Does he mean to send us to Antwerp?'

'No, he says we must go to England, and he intends to come with us.'

She did not wish to go, she knew, while the

earl was here. She had heard no more from him, and worried that his injuries and exertions on their behalf could have been too much for him. Tomorrow, she decided, she would visit his lodgings and ask after him.

That evening Sir William told them more of his plans.

'Some of the men we have here, who are not badly wounded, can now leave and go back to their regiments. The rest can be taken to Madame Antoine's, she already has a small hospital set up in her ballroom, and says she will be glad to take them. We will organize that tomorrow, and the following day, unless Sir Henry has a relapse, we will set out towards the coast. We will take it easily. Jeanette and the others here can clean the house, for I am giving up the lease. I have had word the Foreign Office will soon be sending me somewhere else.'

'We'll need two carriages,' Sally said. 'There must be room for Henry to stretch out and sleep if he needs to.'

'I'm seeing to all that. You girls, start your packing.'

Phoebe tossed all night. She must see the earl, and make sure he was recovering. It might be considered forward of her, but she cared nothing for that. She would go to his rooms in the morning. It would be the last time she would ever see him, most likely, but she could not leave without knowing he was on the mend.

She slipped out early the next day, saying she had shopping to do. The city was still in disarray, but a little progress had been made in finding shelter for the wounded and burying the dead. When she knocked on the door of the earl's lodgings, she was holding her breath, wondering if he was here. His valet opened the door and for a moment she was unable to speak. At least he was still here.

'How . . . how is the earl?' she managed at last.

'You were the young lady who brought him home?' the man asked, belatedly recognizing her. 'But you were — that is — '

'Yes, I was wearing breeches,' Phoebe said, seeing his embarrassment. 'I — we felt it would be safer when we went out to the battlefield. How is he?'

'Better now, miss. The wound became infected, and for some days he was delirious, and if there had been surgeons available he might have lost the leg. All they can think of is amputation,' he added bitterly.

'Oh, no! But how is he? Is he better?'

The man laughed. 'Of course. I've tended wounds before, I was with him in the

Peninsula. He's almost himself again, and just this minute threw the bowl of gruel I'd prepared for his breakfast at me, demanding a steak.'

Phoebe laughed. 'Then I hope you'll provide him with a steak.'

'If he's fit enough to want one, of course I will. I'll be glad to see him regaining his strength. My next job is to persuade him to go back home.'

'Does he wish to go home?'

'He needs to, to recover in peace. But will you come and see him? Was that what you wanted?'

'I — yes, please.'

He led the way upstairs to the rooms the earl occupied, and ushered Phoebe into the bedroom, where the earl, propped up on pillows, was glaring in the direction of the door.

'Is that my steak?' he demanded, and then saw Phoebe. His expression changed from annoyance to an amazed welcome. 'Phoebe?'

She wanted to throw herself on the bed and take him in her arms, but could do no more than shake her head and sink into the chair set beside the bed. He looked pleased to see her, and that was all she cared about.

He stretched out a hand to clasp hers. 'Bring some coffee. The steak can wait.'

Phoebe heard the door close softly behind her, but her whole attention was on the earl.

'You shouldn't have come back with us, looking for Henry,' she said, 'it must have made your wound worse.'

'How could I have let you go through that horror alone? Phoebe, are you all right?'

She laughed unsteadily. 'Of course I am. And Henry is better. What of you? Your man says you have been desperately ill.'

'It's over now, and I'll soon be up and about if that nanny will give me some proper food. And then — ' He stopped, and looked deep into her eyes. 'Oh, Phoebe, we should be in a moonlit garden, listening to soft music, with the scent of flowers all about us. How the devil can a man propose when he's lying in a sickbed, too weak to get to his feet and take you in his arms?'

She swallowed. 'Propose, my lord?'

'My name is Zachary. I want you to call me that. Phoebe, my darling, I made a mull of it last time. Letting you think all I cared about was for a son to deprive Jonas and his misbegotten sons of my title. No, listen to me,' he said as she tried to speak, 'I don't care if you give me a dozen daughters, or none at all. I want you for my wife, that is all. If we are blessed with children, I will welcome them, but I don't need them to be utterly content with you. Lying here, I've been making plans. You will love my home, and there is a very pretty dower house where your mother can live, if she chooses. I can't imagine she enjoys being with Mr Bradshaw.'

Before she could reply the valet entered with a tray on which there were coffee cups, a pot of the fragrant brew, some soft new rolls, butter and conserves.

'Your breakfast, sir, madam,' he said, placing the tray on a table beside the bed. 'Perhaps madam will pour?'

Phoebe, who had tried to snatch her hand away from the earl's grasp when the valet entered, nodded.

'Leave it to me, and I'll make sure your master has something to eat. Perhaps he could have the steak for dinner?'

The man smiled and backed out of the room. Phoebe again tried to free her hand. 'I can't pour the coffee,' she pointed out.

'You are not going to pour it until you say you'll be my wife. Phoebe, whenever I've been in my senses these past days I've been dreaming of holding you in my arms, wishing you to come to me. Will you marry me? Please?'

'Of course I will, if only to make you drink your coffee.'

'Be damned to the coffee!'

With surprising strength he pulled her towards him, and she found herself sitting on the side of the bed, clasped in his arms, and being ruthlessly kissed.

'I'll be fit to travel in a few days. Will you trust yourself to me, and I'll take you back to Beatrice? She'll be only too delighted to arrange the wedding. Can it be soon? You don't want to spend months gathering a trousseau, do you?'

'Sir William plans to leave in a day or so, taking Henry home. You could come with us, which would be easier for you. Oh, Zachary, I'm so thankful to find you getting better!' she said, and burst into tears. 'I was so frightened for you!'

He soothed her, kissed her eyes, wiped her tears away with a corner of the sheet, and eventually agreed to let her go so that they could drink the rather cold coffee, and she could butter the rolls and feed them to him.

Then she had to exert all her will to prevent him when he said he was strong enough to dress and escort her back to Sir William's house.

'I can't risk a relapse,' she said, kissing him. 'I will make arrangements, and come to tell you of them this afternoon, and we will be able to set off in a few days. Oh, my dear love,

I want you well and strong again. I love you so much.'

'For you, I'll endure gruel if it brings our wedding forward. Come here, kiss me again, or I might imagine I'm still delirious and it's not really happening.'

'It's real, my love,' she said as she sat once more on the bed and clasped him in her arms, surrendering to his kisses.

We do hope that you have enjoyed reading this large print book.

Did you know that all of our titles are available for purchase?

We publish a wide range of high quality large print books including:
Romances, Mysteries, Classics
General Fiction
Non Fiction and Westerns

Special interest titles available in large print are:
The Little Oxford Dictionary
Music Book
Song Book
Hymn Book
Service Book

Also available from us courtesy of Oxford University Press:
Young Readers' Dictionary
(large print edition)
Young Readers' Thesaurus
(large print edition)

For further information or a free brochure, please contact us at:
Ulverscroft Large Print Books Ltd.,
The Green, Bradgate Road, Anstey,
Leicester, LE7 7FU, England.
Tel: (00 44) 0116 236 4325
Fax: (00 44) 0116 234 0205